BUTTERFINGERS

BUTTER

J. M.
Trewellard

FINGERS

Illustrated by Ian Beck

David Fickling Books

OXFORD · NEW YORK

For my sons,
Joseph and Edward Trewellard,
and with thanks to Zoe Allday.

J. M. TREWELLARD

A DAVID FICKLING BOOK

Published by David Fickling Books
an imprint of Random House Children's Books
a division of Random House, Inc.
New York

DAVID FICKLING BOOKS and colophon are trademarks of David Fickling.

www.randomhouse.com/kids

Educators and librarians, for a variety of teaching tools,
visit us at www.randomhouse.com/teachers

Library of Congress Cataloging-in-Publication Data
Trewellard, Juliet.
Butterfingers / Juliet Trewellard ; illustrated by Ian Beck. — 1st American ed.
p.   cm.
SUMMARY: When beautiful Princess Bella is kidnapped by a fearsome dragon,
it is left to a clumsy stable boy, accompanied by his dog and pony, to save her.
ISBN 978-0-385-75123-0 (trade)—ISBN 978-0-385-75124-7 (lib. bdg.)
[1. Dragons—Fiction. 2. Princesses—Fiction. 3. Clumsiness—Fiction.
4. Animals—Fiction. 5. Fairy tales.] I. Beck, Ian, ill. II. Title.
PZ8.T773Bu 2007
[Fic]—dc22   2006038479

Printed in the United States of America

10 9 8 7 6 5 4 3 2 1

First American Edition

NED

ON A GREEN HILL STOOD A KING'S PALACE, SURROUNDED BY THE ROLLING HILLS, FIELDS AND WOODS WHICH WERE HIS KINGDOM. Inside the palace lived the king with his daughter, the lovely Princess Bella. Her beauty delighted all who set eyes on her. Outside there were large formal gardens with knot-hedges and herbs and roses of all kinds. There were tree-lined walks and arches and mazes. There were small secret gardens with seats and arbours. The towers of the palace reached high up into the sky.

Today it was clear and very blue. There was nothing in it but a few fluffy clouds, until suddenly several large black and white birds appeared, calling harshly to each other. They were magpies. They flew steadily over the king's land, looking down on the neat meadows and moats that surrounded the palace.

The birds soared over the courtyard, the gardens and the stables – a long stone building with rows of neat, wide stalls for the king's fine horses. One magpie soared lower, spying the tiny figure of a stableboy.

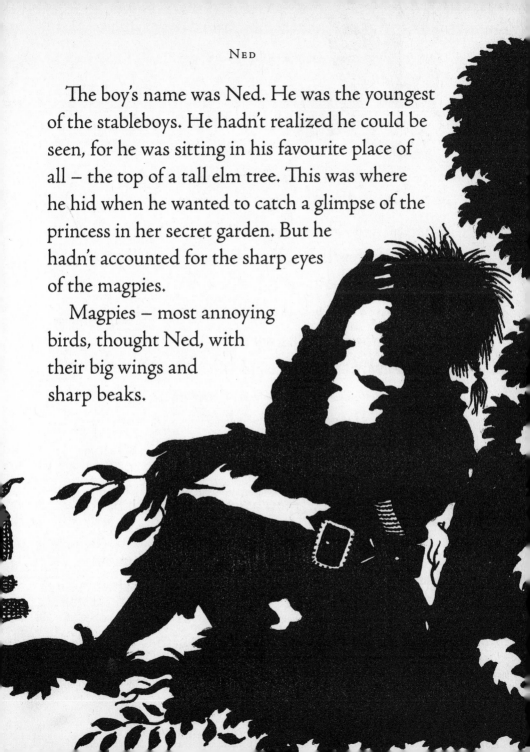

The boy's name was Ned. He was the youngest
of the stableboys. He hadn't realized he could be
seen, for he was sitting in his favourite place of
all – the top of a tall elm tree. This was where
he hid when he wanted to catch a glimpse of the
princess in her secret garden. But he
hadn't accounted for the sharp eyes
of the magpies.

Magpies – most annoying
birds, thought Ned, with
their big wings and
sharp beaks.

Always interfering in other people's business, always making trouble. Nosy, and greedy: their beady eyes were always looking out for precious objects which they could take back to their nests as trophies. Nothing bright or shiny was safe when a magpie was around.

"Cack-cack-cack, Clumsy!" Ned jumped and almost toppled from the tree. "I know you, Butterfingers. Skiving again!" cackled the magpie, and swooped a little lower.

"Go away, Magpie," said Ned.

"Cack-cack-cack, you'll never amount to anything, Butterfingers."

"Be quiet, Magpie," called up Ned, "and don't call me that name."

But the magpie merely laughed and flapped his wings, soaring up to join the other birds. As he flew, he eyed the martins, which flew in and out of their nests under the eaves of the stables.

"You keep away from those martins' nests,"

called Ned to the big bird. "I've seen you steal their eggs. You're a thief!"

"Quiet, boy. Get back to dreaming," called the others.

"Cack-cack-cack!" laughed the magpies, their wings flapping. "Nothing for you, boy, but work and dreams, work and dreams." And they flew off.

"Look sharp, lad!" barked Tuff. "Dreaming again! Back to work, boy, for goodness' sake! Don't want old grumble-guts, Mr Squelch, after you!"

Tuff was Ned's little dog. Now he stood at the bottom of the tree, yapping and looking cross. Ned lost his footing on the last branch and slid to the ground in a rush.

"I don't know, boy," Tuff said. "What am I to do with you? When will you ever learn? I thought you'd get a little less clumsy as you grew older, but bless me, the longer your legs are, the more you trip over them. And what have you been up to? Spying on the princess?"

"I wasn't spying," said Ned, getting up. "Just trying to find a bit of peace and quiet."

"No chance of that, lad, if you annoy the stable master!"

Ned ignored his little dog. He was used to him grumbling on. Tuff had been with Ned since he was a pup. He was a grumbly sort of dog even then, but they were used to each other.

Ned hurried off to his work in the stables. As usual, there was a lot to do.

"That's my good boy," came the soft voice of Dilly, the pony who was stabled in the far corner. "Back to work." Dilly was not much good for anything but pulling carts, but Ned loved her. He slept on the straw by her stall at night. Tuff slept with him, curled up at his side, or sometimes on his tummy – until he got too heavy and Ned pushed him off. Tuff, the brown and white terrier, and Dilly, the little bay mare – these were Ned's only friends. He looked after them – or was it the other way round? Dilly thought him

wonderful. Didn't he bring her extra rations?
Wasn't he always kind to her? He was her boy, he
was. "My Ned," she'd say, "is a good, kind boy.
And good, kind boys get their rewards eventually.
And my Ned will, you mark my words."

SQUELCH

SQUELCH, THE STABLE MASTER, WAS SHOUTING AS USUAL. He had a lot of work to do, for all the knights had been at a tournament and had brought their horses back hot and dirty. The grooms were running back and forth, trying not to upset Squelch. It didn't take much. He was sitting on a bench in the yard, scowling and wiping his red face with a handkerchief, tired from all his yelling. His large stomach hung over his belt and he looked out of breath. Now he spotted Ned.

"Go and get my dinner, boy, and don't take all day about it!" he shouted.

Ned headed for the kitchen, dawdling

as he went. It seemed sensible to walk slowly, for all around him were knights clanking about in their armour, or grooms running to take horses from them. He sidled around the edge of the yard, keeping out of everyone's way. Above him, chattering maids were shaking sheets out of windows. Three chickens scuttled across in front of him, squawking loudly, and Ned nearly tripped over them! As he watched them pecking at the ground, he noticed clumps of violets growing there, bright purple against the stone. Ned leaned against the wall, enjoying the sun on his face. It was no good; he'd better get on.

He went and hovered by the kitchen door. The cook, looking very large in her white apron, shook her spoon at him.

"Late again, idle Ned. Here – get the tray and take this pie – it's hot from the oven – and that jug of ale to Mr Squelch double quick!"

Ned picked up the tray carefully, left the kitchen by way of the herb garden and crossed to the courtyard. Tuff, scowling, trotted up to him.

"Hurry up, Ned! Don't make the stable master angry again!"

"Out of my way, Tuff," said Ned. "This tray's heavy." Tuff ignored him, nipping at his heels. Ned held the tray carefully, one finger curled round the handle of the jug for extra safety. Then he heard the sound of laughter, bell-like, across the yard.

Ned turned his head and saw, beyond the lawn, the princess with her maid. His tray wobbled.

"Watch it, lad," said Tuff. "Hurry up!"

Now a large shire horse was being led out of the yard by two grooms. The horse pranced about, its large feet coming dangerously close. Ned cleverly side-stepped to avoid them and carried on. But now he saw a flock of geese, honking and waddling across his path. Was there ever a busier day? Tuff was, as usual, almost under his feet. The tray tilted and the pie-dish slid to one side.

"Who-ooa!" Ned quickly righted it and carried on.

"For goodness' sake, lad," said Tuff.

"I'm all right! Stop fussing and get out of my way."

Ned walked as carefully as he could; he was nearly there. He concentrated hard, keeping an eye out for the chickens, which were still wandering about. As he watched a little yellow chick hurrying to catch up with its mother, he suddenly saw a pair of shiny pointed shoes and the edge of a white dress. His head came up quickly and his heart gave a thump. The princess was crossing his path, laughing with her maid! It was only for a moment, just a second – yet how close he was to her!

She glanced at him, her blue eyes bright under very long lashes. She gave a little smile and then she was gone, hurrying towards the stables, still laughing.

Ned stopped dead, suddenly breathless, and turned his head to watch her. Tuff, hurrying after him, scuttled between his feet.

"Oh, Tuff! Get away!" said Ned. But – bang! –

he bumped into a corner of the wall. As if with a will of its own, the tray tipped: the ale seemed to jump out of the jug and onto Ned's clothes, and the pie slithered out of its dish and down Ned's skinny legs, breaking up as it went and spilling gravy all over Ned's feet and the ground.

Mr Squelch, who had been watching the progress of his pie and ale as they crossed the courtyard, now got heavily to his feet and made his way over.

Whack! He cuffed Ned across the head.

"You stupid butterfingers! Look what you've done! Careless, clumsy oaf! Go back to the kitchen and get me another dinner – quick!"

"Sorry, Mr Squelch." Ned, slipping in the gravy as he went, picked up the tray and the pie-dish; the jug was broken.

"I said quick!" yelled Squelch.

Ned ran back to the kitchen. Tuff, ashamed, slunk after him.

The cook took one look at Ned, covered in ale and gravy, and whacked him once round the face with her dishcloth, and once on the head with her wooden spoon. Watching from the doorway, Tuff winced in sympathy.

"Butterfingers!" screamed Cook. "Idle, clumsy boy! Can't concentrate on a thing! Can't do the simplest job without making a mess! Look at my jug – broken! Look at my pie – ruined!"

Ned sighed. He turned once more to look for the princess, but she had long gone. He turned back to Tuff. "Please don't call me Butterfingers" was all he said.

Later, from the stables, Ned heard Sir Pevner, one of the king's knights, shouting out. Of all the king's knights, he was the bravest and the strongest. Ned gazed at him in admiration as he came striding across the courtyard, clanking in his suit of chain mail. He had piercing blue eyes and long dark hair. He had broad shoulders and he was very tall. He seemed to tower over Ned. "Fetch me my sword from the arms room," he said. "I'm off for a spot of sword practice."

"Yes, sir," said Ned, and ran across the stable yard to the arms room, which was full of pieces of armour, bright helmets with plumes, spears and sharp, shiny swords. Ned would have liked to try on a helmet and buckle on a sword, but Sir Pevner was waiting.

A boy with ginger hair handed the sword to him. "You take care of this, Butterfingers," he said, grinning. "It's sharp, you know. Don't want to cut yourself, do you?"

Ned didn't say anything, but Tuff growled menacingly at the boy as his master grabbed the heavy sword and ran out.

Ned held the sword
firmly in his hand.
How the sun glinted on
it. Swish, swish – he practised
sword thrusts as he crossed the yard.
He made imaginary stabs. He parried.
He wished he was a knight. The sword felt
heavy in his skinny arm, but he felt brave and
strong. That was what mattered. He stood a little
taller and held it firmly.

"Bring it here, boy," called Sir Pevner. Ned
jumped guiltily and the sword clattered to the
ground. "Swords aren't to be mucked about with,
lad. It's not a toy, you know."

Ned reddened and ran forward to give the knight his sword. Sir Pevner strode off. Ned sighed. He wondered if he would ever be that important.

As he strolled slowly back towards the stables, followed, as usual, by Tuff, the violets he'd spotted earlier caught his eye again. On impulse he bent down and picked some.

"What you doing now, boy?" asked Tuff.

"Look at these violets. Aren't they an amazing colour? When I'm a knight, I'll have a rich violet shield."

"Hmmph!" grunted Tuff scornfully. "A flower-picking knight?!"

"Very pretty, dear," said Dilly, who had come out to meet them.

"Don't you encourage him, you old mare," snapped Tuff.

Ned sighed and stuffed the bunch of violets in his hat.

"He's at that age," Dilly told Tuff.

"Hmmph!" said Tuff again. "My goodness, boy. Don't know which is worse – playing at being a knight, or picking flowers. Flowers! You're as daft as a brush!"

THE BUNCH OF VIOLETS

NED WAS BUSY FILLING A NOSEBAG WITH OATS WHEN HE HEARD A COMMOTION OUT IN THE COURTYARD. It was the Princess Bella!

She had come to ride her horse. How lovely she looked, standing in the sunshine with her maid, somehow shining and bright and – like a flower, thought Ned.

Squelch hurried forward, concerned. The princess usually only rode in the exercise yard with her riding master.

"What an honour, m'lady!" he said. "But where is your riding master? The king gave orders—"

Bella held her head high.
"I've decided to go for a ride.
Saddle my horse
quickly, please."

Squelch's face
assumed a smiling
grimace and he bowed
deeply, his large stomach
pushing against his legs.
Ned heard Bella and her maid
giggle as they turned their faces
away.

Squelch bellowed at Ned, "Quick,
boy!" but Ned was gazing at the princess.

"Loafer!" screamed the stable master. "Move!
Saddle! Princess waiting! Double quick!"

Ned blinked and then hurried into the stable
to look for the saddle. He glanced back at the
princess. The sunlight made her hair flash like
gold. Now, where was the saddle? As he picked
up a brown leather one, the little dog, Tuff,

squeezed through under the half-door.

"Not that one, stupid!" he hissed. "The silver one with the red tassels! Quick, Ned! Up there on the shelf! What would you do without me, eh?"

Ned ran up the wooden ladder. It shook and swayed and then toppled. He reached out a hand to seize the saddle and promptly fell down with it on top of him.

Squelch was making polite conversation with the princess.

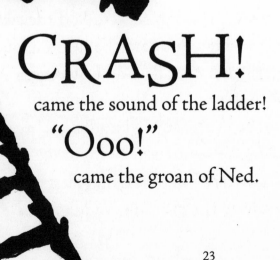

CRASH!

came the sound of the ladder!

"Ooo!"

came the groan of Ned.

"Butterfingers!" muttered Master Squelch furiously under his breath.

"Get up quick, you great lummox! The saddle!" Tuff yapped urgently.

Really, Ned felt he could do nothing right today. He saw the princess waiting. On an impulse he took the bunch of violets out of his hat and fastened them to the pommel of the heavy saddle. As he ran back, Tuff woofed, "Stand straight, boy! Meeting royalty, you know! Keep your head!"

"Get that dog out of the way!" rapped out the stable master. "And hurry up, boy!"

Ned hurried. The sun reflected off the silver edges of the saddle. Suddenly he heard a loud cackle and the magpies flew down towards the glinting silver.

"Not you again," said Ned under his breath. "Go away."

"Cack-cack-cack," went the magpies, hopping nearer, drawn to the gleaming saddle. One cocked his head to one side and looked up, spying the bright necklace around the princess's throat.

Ned heaved the silver saddle onto the princess's horse.

"Not that way, boy – oh, give it here!" snapped the stable master. He took it from Ned, turned it round and fastened it himself, crushing the violets as he did so.

"Get!" he said, half under his breath, jerking his head in the direction of the stables. He aimed a sharp kick at Ned, who started to scuttle off.

"Boy," came a voice. Ned turned and saw that the princess was looking at him.

"Thank you very much. I like violets," she said, staring at him with her forget-me-not blue eyes and giving him a big smile. What could he do but smile back?

Bella carefully took the half-crushed bunch of violets and tucked them into her belt. "Thank you," she said again. Then, with a little spring, she mounted her horse and grinned down at her maid. "Really, why can't they let me wear breeches?" she said in an undertone. "Then see how fast I could ride."

Her maid laughed. "I'm not joking," said Bella. "Now – no telling, Joan. I'll see you in a while. You've no idea where I am."

"Right you are," said Joan cheerfully. Bella turned her horse round, but as she did so, she gave Ned a wink and another wide smile.

Ned stood and watched her riding off. His heart had given a big leap in his chest and he felt as if he would grin for ever.

"Cack-cack-cack," came the scornful laugh of a magpie. "Nothing for you but work and dreams."

But Ned didn't care. He leaned against Dilly's warm flank and smiled up at her.

"She's very lovely, dear," said Dilly, "but not for the likes of you."

"What?" snapped Tuff, jumping up and down on his little legs. "What? Wouldn't even look at you, that one! Wouldn't even give you the time of day, let alone speak to you. You remember your station, me boy!"

"She did speak to me," said Ned. "She said she liked violets. And she said thank you."

"Here we go," said Tuff. "The boy's dreamy again. Well, wake up sharp, Ned, lad, for I spy an angry Squelch marching through the door, and he's coming this way!"

THE GOLDEN BALL

AFTER THAT, NED CLIMBED THE ELM MORE OFTEN AND WATCHED THE PRINCESS PLAYING HAPPILY IN HER GARDEN, BUT SHE NEVER SAW HIM. The sun moved slowly across the courtyard. The martins flashed in and out of their nests under the eaves. Their chicks flew the nest and chanced the sky, often clinging to the walls of the outhouses with their tiny feet before dropping and then finding their wings again. The greedy magpies, on the lookout for baby birds, were shooed away by Ned and Tuff, and all seemed well.

"Sometimes life is very peaceful, isn't it, Dilly?"

said Ned, enjoying the sunshine on his face. "But when I'm a man, I'll be a knight; then I'll have adventures."

"Yes, dear," said Dilly. "Time enough for that."

The seeds of the dandelion clocks drifted across and time seemed to pass slowly. Then one day the palace came alive, with running servants, a fanfare of trumpets and hundreds of doves let loose in the bright sky. The magpies, watching from the roof, almost fell off in surprise. It was Princess Bella's birthday.

Ned watched from his corner in the stable yard and sighed as the princess came out into the sunshine. She was dressed in a long, heavy velvet gown, and she was making a determined effort to walk in a lady-like way. She held up the hem of her dress and stepped forward to meet her father.

Now the king came out into the main courtyard, followed by courtiers and pageboys. Beckoning to a small boy, he told him to take a present to the Princess Bella. Ned was impressed

by the page's velvet breeches and fine buckled
shoes. He absent-mindedly rubbed one of
his old shoes against the back of his leg as he
watched. He frowned up at the magpies as they
hopped across the tiles to get a better view.

But before he could do anything, the page
came forward bearing a red cushion on which
was placed a beautiful ball, bright and shining,
made of the finest meshed gold, yet light and
fine to throw. It flashed in the sunlight.

"Oh!" exclaimed the princess. "It's just what I
wanted! How did you know, Father? A perfect
size for a game of catch." She rushed forward
to take the ball, yanking up the skirt of her
dress in her haste. The king raised his
eyes to the sky.

Picking up the ball, Bella threw
it high into the air, twirled, and
caught it again with one hand
behind her back. The crowd
cheered.

Then down flew the magpies, one, two, three, looking excited. They eyed the bright golden ball and fluttered as close as they dared, but nobody seemed to notice them, except Ned.

While everyone else was looking at the princess, he ran out and flapped his cleaning leather at them furiously, finally shooing them off.

Early the next morning,
before he was sent on his
errands, Ned climbed his
favourite tree again. He sat on a
tall branch, feeling the gentle wind in
the leaves, watching the birds fly past
and seeing people starting to stir below.
The day was beginning. He had a few
moments before he was summoned.

He loved the early morning, when the sky
was fresh and clear. But today he saw a dark
cloud to the west, sitting heavily over the horizon.
A strange wind blew through the garden and
rustled the leaves of his tree.

He heard the little click of the gate to the
secret garden and, to his very great delight, saw
the princess come in. She walked down a path
lined with lavender, and as she brushed against it,
Ned smelled its sweet scent.

When she reached the lawn in the centre of
the garden, she took out her new golden ball.

Ned knew he shouldn't be spying, but he just loved watching her. Indeed, the whole garden seemed hushed, expectant, as Bella threw up the ball and caught it again. But then, her face turned upwards to catch the ball, she saw the magpies fly overhead.

"Bother," she said out loud. "I hope they aren't going to spoil my fun. I never get any proper time to practise."

"Cack-cack-cack," shrieked the largest bird. "Watch out – you're being spied on!"

They swooped down near Ned, who almost lost
his hold on the tree trunk.

"What? Oh, it's you, the violets boy! Hello!"
said Bella. "Here – catch!" She threw her ball up,
sure and straight, towards him. He ducked and
the ball soared over him and down again, while
the princess raced round and caught it in one
hand.

"Oooh!" cried Ned. Now he totally lost his
balance and toppled out of the elm, falling on
the grass with a bump. He sat there, his spiky
hair falling over his eyes, and rubbed his elbow.
"Ouch," he said, looking up at the princess's
laughing face. "I'm sorry, my lady, really I am. It's
just . . . that's my favourite tree."

"Hmm, skiving, no doubt."

"Oh no, my lady, I—"

"I didn't mean to laugh at you," said the
princess. "But you did look rather funny toppling
out of the tree. Did you hurt yourself?" she asked,
coming closer.

Ned leaped to his feet. "No, no, I'm fine, my lady."

"Good," said Bella. She studied his face, her eyes twinkling, then gave him a big smile. "Well, as you're here you can play ball with me. I normally have to play on my own." She ran into the centre of the lawn. "Here," she yelled cheerfully. "Catch!"

Ned hurtled towards the ball with his arm outstretched. The ball hit his hand. "Ouch," he said, and dropped it on the grass.

"Butterfingers," said the princess. But she smiled at him.

The magpies settled on the bushes and jeered at Ned.

"Oh come on, never mind them. Pick it up. Throw it to me!" said Bella.

Ned lobbed it towards her. It flew hopelessly wide, but she launched herself sideways like a goalkeeper, caught it in one hand, rolled over in one easy movement and came up again, laughing.

Ned gazed at her open-mouthed. "You're amazing," he said.

"Thank you," she said. "You're not much good at catching or throwing, are you? Never mind, you'll get better with practice. Meanwhile, it's all the better practice for me. This is fun!"

The magpies flew down from the bushes and hopped nearer, watching the ball greedily with their beady eyes.

The princess threw the ball up high in the air and caught it again. "Watch me throw this right over that tall fir and catch

it on the other side," she called to Ned. She
lobbed the ball even higher and started
to run round the tree. Ned watched
the golden ball as it gleamed and
glittered in the sunlight. But
before it had a chance to fall, a
huge shadow came over them,
causing even the magpies to flutter
away in alarm.

A vast dark shape was above
them! It had outstretched
wings like a swirling black
cape. There was a hiss
and then a roar! The
whole sky seemed
blotted out for
a moment
and the sun
dimmed.

Smoke filled the garden. Then, in a
sudden rush of air, the princess was
lifted up, caught in a claw, her small
feet dangling. Her pale dress
shone against the darkness of the
outstretched wings. Her eyes were
wide, her hands imploring, her lips
parted. High, high she went.

Horrified, Ned stood stock-still,
staring. He didn't know what had
happened. Something huge and
black was soaring upwards with
his beautiful princess; they
were somehow locked
together in a whirl
and a scream!

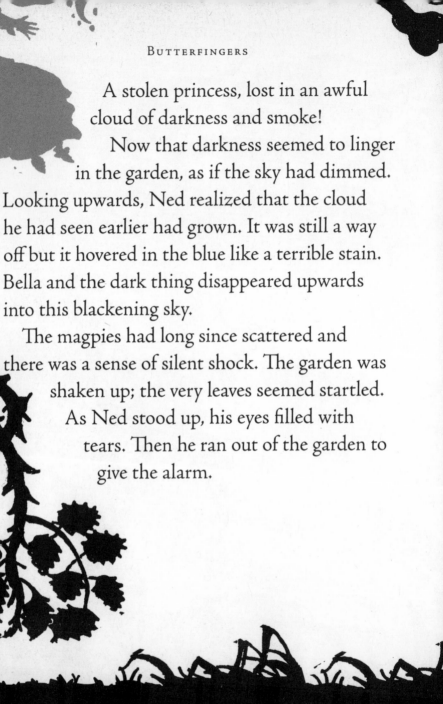

A stolen princess, lost in an awful
cloud of darkness and smoke!

Now that darkness seemed to linger
in the garden, as if the sky had dimmed.
Looking upwards, Ned realized that the cloud
he had seen earlier had grown. It was still a way
off but it hovered in the blue like a terrible stain.
Bella and the dark thing disappeared upwards
into this blackening sky.

The magpies had long since scattered and
there was a sense of silent shock. The garden was
shaken up; the very leaves seemed startled.

As Ned stood up, his eyes filled with
tears. Then he ran out of the garden to
give the alarm.

There was nothing, then, in the secret garden, but the shaking bushes and the bruised flowers. And a bright golden ball, which rolled

slowly upon the grass as Princess Bella's cry was lost in the air.

THE SHADOW-CLOUD

NED SPREAD THE ALARM ABOUT THE PALACE AND SOON PEOPLE WERE RUNNING PAST HIM, YELLING FOR THE KNIGHTS. All was confusion and fear. What terrible monster had stolen the princess? Ned went over and over in his head the moment when the princess had been lifted upwards before his very eyes. Oh, why hadn't he caught hold of her and saved her? Why had he just stared, doing nothing until it was too late?

He stood helpless while all the court seethed and fretted around him. A wind rustled around

the stable yard, lifting a blade of straw. Ned
watched it move across the courtyard and stir
the trees beyond. He raised his eyes to the sky
and saw, to his horror, the dark cloud spreading,
bringing with it a long trail of mist. It was still
some way off, but it hung threateningly in the sky.

In the distance the green fields and the yellow
corn changed colour as the cloud moved over
them and the dogs started to howl. Ned suddenly
felt fearful and scuttled back to the stables,
tripping as he went and upsetting the buckets
and hay forks in a clatter.

Tuff came running out to meet him. "Quick,
lad! Something's happening!"

Into the courtyard came the king's men,
preceded by two trumpeters, who stood side by
side and gave long blasts from their trumpets.
Then the knights lined up, followed by the lords
and ladies of the court, the kitchen staff, the
stable master and the grooms – all stood outside
to listen to the king's pronouncement.

Finally the king appeared before them.

"In the light of the terrible disaster that has befallen us, I ask my knights to go forth, rescue our beloved Princess Bella and save our kingdom!"

The people standing around murmured to each other. Tuff pressed himself against Ned's legs.

"And to lead this quest, we look to our champion knight, Sir Pevner." The tall knight came forward and knelt down. "Find the monster and destroy him," the king went on. "Restore the Princess Bella to us – send word quickly to let me know she is safe. If all is well, send one of the doves."

Sir Pevner stood and bowed his head.

The king started for the palace, then turned back to add quietly, "But if all is ill, send a hawk. Let us pray you have only need of a dove."

As soon as the king and all the lords and ladies and heralds and footmen had returned to the palace, Ned heard Squelch yelling his orders, and soon the boy was rushing to prepare the horses. How he wished he was getting ready to ride out himself. Sir Cuthbert was trying to get everyone in order. "Come along, come along! Get in line. Heads up, helmets straight! Out of the way, stupid boy!"

"Get that boy out of the way, Squelch," yelled Sir Belwyn, as Ned dodged in front of him. "I won't have that boy around these horses. He's too clumsy. Back to the stables, boy, and quick!"

Ned did as he was told, and watched the proud knights from a distance. Their heavy swords clanked by their sides and their banners flew and their drummers drummed and their bright shields flashed.

At the head of the procession was Sir Pevner. His long dark hair flowed from under his shiny helmet and he carried a silver shield embossed with a red lion – the king's emblem. His white charger tossed its proud head up and down while it waited. Sir Pevner's eyes gazed ahead, and in his hand he held a long silver sword, also engraved with a lion.

The champion knight pointed his sword
ahead – the sign for all to move forward. The
horses' hooves clattered on the stones; thin grey
dogs ran by their side. The pale sunlight glinted
on the knights' armour and they left the palace
walls with a clatter and a blast of trumpets. Not
one knight faltered or looked back.

"Didn't Sir Pevner look brave, Tuff? What a huge sword. He'll be bound to find the princess and kill the monster, won't he?" said Ned.

"Let's hope so, lad," muttered Tuff as he sat at Ned's side watching them go. "This is a pretty pickle."

Ned stood leaning on his broom. "How empty it is in the stables now," he said.

"A bit of peace and quiet," said the little brown and white dog, "without all them show-off chargers, tossing their heads, demanding the best of everything. Still, they've got a hard task ahead of them, no doubt."

"Waste of time! Waste of time!" cackled the magpies circling above.

"They might as well send you, Butterfingers," one called, "for all the use it'd be."

They laughed. "Waste of time," they called as they flew off.

Ned sighed. He wished he could go with the knights to rescue the princess and save the kingdom. But he was just a stable lad and odd-job boy. What could he do?

"Best get to work, Ned dear," said Dilly, coming out to join them.

"How can you think about work, Dilly, when the princess has been stolen by a monster? I must help find her!"

"Don't be stupid, boy," yapped Tuff. "We're not members of the court. Rescuing and fighting – we can't do that. Things like that have to be left to knights. You listen to me, boy. There's nothing a lad like you can do."

TREASURE

NED COULDN'T STOP WORRYING. He couldn't help but think of the princess: her big grin; her clever tricks with the ball; the way she spoke to him; a little sharp, yes, he had to admit that, but also – Ned suddenly smiled at the memory – it was also rather . . . friendly.

Then one day, as he stood leaning against the wall, thinking of Bella, he saw, soaring over the courtyard and into a palace window, one of the knights' hawks!

This brought deep anxiety throughout the kingdom. The hawk was a sign that the knights

were in trouble,
perhaps all dead.
A sense of
hopelessness
lay in the
hearts of all the
people. And in the
distance the dark cloud was a constant reminder
that all was not well. The king sat silent on his
throne. He refused the food the servants brought
him; he refused to talk to the lords and ladies.
Yet, in the mornings, he would rise and walk to
the secret garden where Bella had played with her
ball. He would stand at the gate and look in.

The king was not the only one who did this.

Ned had spent his life in secret ways. He was
used to creeping past sleeping stable masters,
avoiding the cooks in the kitchen, sticking to the
corners of the busy yards for fear of getting in the
way, or being told to run here and there, do this,
do that.

Now, in the same secret way, Ned climbed his elm tree to look at the princess's garden. He saw the king leave and walk heavily back to his throne room. Suddenly Ned decided to climb down into the garden. Edging his skinny body along an overhanging branch, he dropped to the ground, feeling scared, but somehow thrilled.

He looked about him and suddenly spied a tiny sparkle of light.

Under a low bush, among the withering flowers, Ned saw Bella's golden ball! It must have rolled under the hedge.

He crossed the lawn and picked up the ball, feeling in his hand the smooth roundness that the Princess Bella must have felt before she was taken. The last hand to touch it had been hers. Now it lay in Ned's. The gold caught what little light there was, and before Ned had a chance to hide the ball, five magpies hurtled down, chattering and squawking.

They circled around Ned, their wings flapping

close, their sharp beaks and fierce claws jabbing
dangerously.

"Leave me alone!" he cried.

"Cack-cack-cack! Treasure! Gold!"

The magpies gathered into a close group
and suddenly swooped, their beaks like arrows,
straight down towards the boy!

Shielding his face with his arm, Ned put the
ball in his pocket and ran as fast as he could
towards the tree. He climbed up and jumped
down on the other side. For once he didn't trip
over as he ran and he didn't drop the ball.

The magpies circled the air above him. "You'll
be sorry! You'll be sorry!" they squawked.

Ned leaned against the door inside the stable,
listening to the cackling voices as the magpies
gave up and flew away. He slowly took the golden
ball from his pocket and looked at it. What had
the magpies said? Treasure. Ned looked up at
the sky and saw, far to the west, the strange dark
cloud. A glimmer of an idea came into his mind.

He put the ball firmly in his pocket.

Ned slipped past the grooms and some quarrelling stableboys to Dilly's stall. As usual, Tuff was sitting in the straw beside her.

"Where've you been?" he snapped. "Mooning around as usual?"

Dilly moved over and nuzzled Ned's neck with her soft nose.

"What would you say, my Dilly," he whispered, "if I told you I was to go and look for the princess?"

The pony looked at him in alarm. "What, go out there with that strange sky and all? Don't be

silly, Ned dear. Searching for princesses isn't for the likes of you."

"I must go and help her," said Ned in an urgent voice. "Suppose the monster—"

"Don't start supposing, dear boy. Doesn't do any good, you know. Why, all those brave knights – maybe they're still all right. They could still find her and save her."

"Hmmph," said Tuff. "Where are they, then? And why did they send that hawk?"

"Will you be quiet, Tuff! No point worrying about what we can't change, is there, Ned dear? It's not for the likes of us. As for that cloud, it'll go in its own good time, I guess, like everything does."

"That's where you're wrong, you silly mare," snapped Tuff suddenly. "That's a magic cloud, that is."

Ned leaned against Dilly's soft body and stroked her ears. "I can't stop worrying."

"Darned right to be worried," said Tuff.

"There's some kind of monster out there, destroying everything and—"

"What kind of monster is it?" asked Ned.

"Well . . . it can fly . . . I don't know . . . it might be a d—"

Dilly gave a nervous little hrrumph.

"No idea, lad," said Tuff quickly. "Tell you straight – and I never thought I'd say this – I'll be glad when those noisy knights and horses are back and things get busy round here again."

"Do you think they will be back?" asked Ned.

"Who knows? Who knows, Ned, lad?" Tuff sat down and started scratching. It always made him feel better.

"There's no one left but us," said Ned. "There's nothing else for it." He took the golden ball out of his pocket. "Look what I've got."

Tuff leaped to his feet, yapping. "Bless my tail!" he said. "What's our foolish Ned done this time? You've not gone and stolen the princess's ball?"

"Not stolen it. Taken it – for the princess,"

said Ned. He stood up straight and, perhaps
for the first time, he didn't look dreamy and he
didn't look clumsy. He fixed his eyes first on Dilly
and then on Tuff. "We have to go and save the
Princess Bella," he said.

NED'S ARMOUR

AT NED'S WORDS, DILLY STIRRED UNEASILY AND TUFF STARTED TO HOP ABOUT IN EXASPERATION.

"We save a princess?" he barked. "Who do you think we are? Knights?"

"Now you're not thinking straight, Ned dear," said Dilly. "The likes of us can't do anything. We're not part of the court."

"I'm going, Dilly. I've got to go."

"And how are you going to save her?" asked Tuff scornfully. "You got a plan, lad?"

"Er . . ." said Ned.

"Thought not. Now, you listen here . . ."

But Ned didn't stop to listen. He went to the

corner of the stable where he kept his knapsack
with his few belongings and started to search
around for a water bottle. Tuff trotted back
and forth crossly, but Ned took no notice. The
dog then went up to Dilly and said gruffly:
"Downright stupid! Needs his head sorting!
Needs an early night! Needs a talking-to!"

"I think he's set on it," said Dilly in a soft,
worried voice.

"Well, count me out! He can go on his own!"
barked Tuff. "He's come to this silly idea on his
own, ain't he? Well, he can sort it on his own.
Why, he ain't even got a plan."

Ned had disappeared into the kitchen. The
cook was dozing in a chair by the window, making
little snuffling noises. No one else was about. He
crept past her and went into the pantry. Very
quietly he smuggled out three large loaves of bread
and some apples and cheese. There was a big pie
on the shelf. Could he take that? It was worth a
try. Oh, and some very nice-looking buns.

When Ned came back to the stables, Tuff was scowling. The dog and the pony watched him searching about in a corner, muttering to himself: "This might come in useful – oh, look what Sir Fayn left behind on the floor. Ah, more bits left by Sir Thoms . . . all very handy for when the time comes."

"What's the great lummox up to now?" wondered Tuff.

Ned had dressed himself in the odd bits of armour that the knights had discarded in favour of larger, stronger pieces. Over his old jerkin he wore a strange bent breastplate that did not do up; he also had a single gauntlet, one elbow and one knee protector and a huge leather belt. Into this he stuffed his own small knife, which he used for whittling wood and paring apples, then he picked up a strong stick and held it like a lance. He came forward into the light, feeling strong and knight-like, and was astonished to see Tuff rolling about on the floor in helpless laughter.

He looked at Dilly. Even she had a small smile on her face.

"Be quiet, Tuff," said Ned crossly. "You never know, I might need protection."

Strange little wheezy noises came from Tuff's throat. Eventually he stopped rolling about and sat up, blinking away his tears of laughter. "Think those odd bits of armour are going to help, do you, lad?"

"Very sensible, I'm sure, dear," said Dilly kindly.

"Well," said Ned, "sensible or not, I'm going to save the princess."

Tuff stopped laughing and got to his feet. Ned picked up his knapsack. He looked at the dog and the pony and they looked back. Nobody spoke. Then he checked that the golden ball was safely in his pocket and headed for the stable door.

Dilly started to follow him.

"Where are you going?" asked Tuff excitedly, running round the pony's legs.

"If Ned goes, I go. You can come or not. Up to you, dear," said Dilly.

"Don't you go pushing me out of the way, you old mare," snapped Tuff. "If Ned goes, we goes – I've said it all along, ain't I? Foolish boy can't cope on his own. Boy can scarcely put a saddle on straight, let alone fight a monster. Anyone can see that." The little dog scurried after the pony.

Ned stood at the door and smiled at them. Then the three started out across the yard.

If the stable master saw them, he did not care. If the quarrelling lads looked up and noticed, they could not be bothered to yell insults. Just Ned, they thought; just Ned.

So the boy led the pony out of the yard and into the open fields. The little brown and white dog skipped along beside them on his small legs, tail in the air, head up. Ned took a deep breath, squared his shoulders and gazed at the horizon.

Then he slowly climbed onto Dilly's back and patted her neck. "Come, Tuff; come, Dilly," he said. "We're going to save a princess."

They watched as the pale sun tried, with difficulty, to shine through the grey mist. The road leading out of the palace gates seemed to stretch a long way ahead, even beyond the king's lands. All Ned could think about just then was following that road to the source of the black shadow-cloud. That was the only plan he had.

MOOS AND MUD

THE ROAD WOUND AHEAD THROUGH FARM LAND. Following it with their eyes, they could just make out the dark shape of woodland; beyond that were hills and, in the far distance, mountains. They seemed such a long way away. In the sky, far ahead, Ned saw the blot of dark cloud, which seemed to reach out into the horizon. He took a deep breath and held Dilly's reins tighter in his hands.

The road was dusty and they could still see traces of the hoof-prints of the knights' horses. Around them was good pastureland, but the fields seemed empty. Then, under a small stand of trees, Ned spied a herd of cows. He called over to them, but they mooed and huddled together.

"What is it, cows?" he called. "We don't mean any harm!"

"Moo-ooo," they all went, jostling around, bumping into each other. They nodded their heads up and down in alarm and their eyes rolled. "Moo-oo-ooo."

Dilly went up to the hedge to neigh a greeting, and one of the cows, a big brown one, turned to look at her. "We're friends, dear," called Dilly.

The cow took a few steps towards her. "Moo – you look friendly, but whoo-oo can tell? It's not safe."

"Moo," all the cows went in unison.

Ned climbed over the hedge and started to walk towards them. "We'll not hurt you, cows. My dog's quite harmless. We're off to fight the monster! Have you seen it?"

The cows now came a little closer. "Monster, monster," they all mooed. "It's dangerous. We stay near the trees. There's this hu-ooo-ge dark monster about. Big as a house."

"Oh," said Dilly in a shaky voice. "Huge and dark, is it?"

"The monster flies over and takes anyone," said the big brown cow in her low, slow voice. She tossed her head up and down sadly. "Some of us were—"

All the cows mooed in loud unison. "Taken, taken—"

"Lifted up, lifted up from our midst, taken," said the brown cow mournfully.

"Lifted up, lifted up," the cows lowed. "Take care, take care!"

A cloud moved over the pale sun and all the cows started to leap about in a panic. "Lo-ook out, loo-ook out!" they warned. "Monster!"

Ned looked up at the sky. "No, no, it's all right, don't panic, cows," he said. "It's only a passing cloud, not the monster or even the shadow-cloud. That's still a long way off."

"Monster, monster . . ." they lowed, backing away.

"No, dears, it's nothing," called Dilly.

"Typical!" said Tuff. "Cows – spooked by nothing! Jump at their own shadows, they would." But just then a very large cow pranced nervously a little too close and Tuff ran behind Ned's legs.

Ned, Tuff and Dilly left the meadow and made their way up the hill past some old farm buildings. There was no one around, but suddenly they heard a snorting and a

squeal. Ned steered Dilly nearer to the wall and looked over. There, lying in a muddy sty, was a large pink pig.

"Oi! Where's my grub?"

"Sorry, Pig, I've no idea. We're just passing through," called Ned over the wall.

"Hummph! Been waiting for my grub for ages. No one's brought it. A disgrace, I say!"

The pig got up from where he'd been wallowing and shuffled over, his large belly rolling a little as he walked.

"What are you up to?"

"We're not up to anything, Pig—" started Ned, but Tuff interrupted: "Save minding our own business! Seems like it wouldn't hurt you to do the same!"

"Ooh, hoity-toity! Only asked so I had some idea of where you were off to.

Considerate, I was. Don't know why I bothered, me so hungry and all. If you want to get yourselves killed, it's no concern of mine."

"Killed?" said Dilly in a shaky voice.

"It's dangerous going about in the daylight now, you know. There's this dreadful winged monster about."

"Oh," said Dilly. "Wings."

"What kind of wings, Pig?" said Ned.

"Big, black, nasty, spiky kind of wings – the sky darkened when that monster went over. I lay down in my sty – a bit muddy, see, and it never saw me. Nasty brute!"

"So it's huge, black and winged!" said Ned, thinking. "Sounds a dangerous beast!"

"I should say so," said Pig. "Best go home and lie low."

"It's the boy – my Ned. He's got some idea of saving the princess," explained Dilly.

"No – don't tell me that awful monster's got the Princess Bella! I don't hear much of the court news out here, you know. You from the court, are you?" said the pig, coming nearer. He blinked at them with his little pink eyes, impressed.

"Oh yeah," said Tuff. "Important members of the court, we are. Oh yeah."

"Be quiet, Tuff," said Ned.

"I've always wanted to meet a court dog," said the pig.

Ned opened his mouth: "We're not members of—" but Tuff interrupted again: "Pleased to meet you too, Pig. You look a good sort."

The pig smiled at Tuff, his little eyes narrowing almost to slits. "Tell you what," he said, "I'll come along. Never know when someone can be of help."

Ned considered it while Tuff watched his face eagerly. After a moment he said: "Thank you. We'd be glad to have you—"

"Tag along!" interrupted Tuff, wagging his tail. "Good-oh. The more the merrier to fight that old monster."

The road veered away from the farm and

wound steadily upwards, getting narrower all the time. The sun, such as it was, lay low in the sky and the shadows deepened. They could see the glint of a river, which ran alongside the road for a while and then seemed to curve away. Ahead of them was a small bridge.

"Come on," said Ned. "We can get to the river bank before nightfall. It seems as good a place as any to rest."

Piggy raised his snout and sniffed. "Might be food ahead," he said, and started to trot a little quicker, snorting loudly through his nose.

The river glinted darkly, the banks edged with

bullrushes and clumps of rough grass. A few
trees leaned over the water and they all settled
down beneath one of these. Ned shared out their
provisions carefully.

"Don't know what the cook will say when she
finds out all her food's gone!" said Dilly.

"Necessary for important court work!" said
Tuff.

Ned and Dilly widened their eyes at each
other.

While Dilly grazed, the others ate the cheese
and some of the pie. But when Piggy started
eyeing the buns, Ned wrapped them up quickly.

"We don't know when we'll get more food," he said. "Got to be careful."

Pig sat down heavily, with a snort. "Not used to all this exercise," he said. "But I can still smell grub."

Tuff put his nose in the air and sniffed. "There's certainly a pong of something, Piggy, old mate," he said.

The river flowed unevenly over small rocks and pebbles, the water tinkling over the stones. Then, as they sat there, they heard the louder sound of a splash!

"Oh, lawks!" grunted Piggy, getting to his feet surprisingly quickly. "It's the monster!"

A POWERFUL PONG OF FISH

DILLY GAVE A LITTLE START BUT NED HELD ON TO HER BRIDLE. "Hang on, Dilly," he said. "I don't think the monster would be in the water."

Tuff had his nose in the air. "It's an animal," he said. "And a strong smell of something."

"Keep quiet!" whispered Ned. "Everyone – ssh!"

Straining their eyes, they saw the shiny head of something swimming downstream. Whatever it was lifted its head and shook it, spraying water around in an

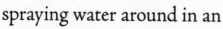

arc. Then, like Tuff, it raised its nose and sniffed.

"Otter," whispered Tuff in a gruff undertone. "Could be a tricky customer." He paused and gave a crooked grin. "Bit fishy, otters – can be a bit slippery." He started to chuckle quietly at his own joke.

Dilly gave a little groan.

"Hush up, Tuff!" hissed Ned. "Let's keep quiet; we need to check if he's friendly. No point in asking for trouble. He's only a little chap but otters have sharp teeth, and there may be more otters with him."

"Well, he could be friendly. One thing's certain . . ." Tuff started to shake again.

"What?"

"There's a powerful pong of fish!"

"Who's there?" asked the otter in a fierce voice. "I smell strangers."

"Friendly strangers," said Tuff, adding under his breath: "He smells strangers? I think he's the smelly one."

Ned stepped forward. "Friends, Mr Otter. Me, Ned, Dilly my pony, Tuff my dog, and our friend Piggy."

"Hmm, a dog. Not too fond of dogs," said the otter gruffly. "Or boys, come to that."

"Oh, we mean no harm, Mr Otter. We're off on a journey. We just stopped for a rest. We've come a long way. Didn't mean to intrude – we can move on, no problem at all."

"Well . . . I guess you can stay and rest a while," said the otter, sounding more friendly now.

"That's very kind of you," said Ned.

"It's nothing," said the otter brusquely. "Welcome. I've a rather small home, but it's all mine, you know. From that bush to this mud slope. Such as it is, it is yours to share while you rest on your journey."

"Thanks," said Piggy. He had found some very tasty mushrooms growing under a bush and settled down happily.

"You know, it's not at all safe to be out and

about these days," said the otter. "There's a monster which terrorizes these parts. It's been known to fly overhead. Terrible times, terrible times. This journey – is it very important? Because if not, I'd advise returning home to the safety of your hearth."

"It is very important," said Ned. "We're—"

"We're off to do a bit of monster-slaying and rescue the princess," said Tuff grandly. "We've come from the court."

"Have you indeed? The court, eh? I heard something about the princess being stolen and saw the knights pass along the road. You don't – forgive my bluntness – you don't look properly equipped for slaying monsters."

"We came away in a bit of a hurry," said Dilly. "We don't really know much about slaying anything, to be honest. We just came with Ned, dear. Where he goes, well, we like to go too, you see. Keep an eye on the boy. He's a good boy, my Ned."

"Well, you'll need a battle strategy – get organized, plan carefully," said the otter, frowning thoughtfully. "I expect you've got it all worked out."

"Er . . ." said Ned.

"Hmmph! Plan!" muttered Tuff. To the otter he said, in a conspiratorial tone, "That boy has never made a plan in—"

Ned moved nearer to the otter, firmly edging Tuff out of the way. "We'd be glad of any information you can give us about this monster," he said. "Best be prepared, I guess."

There was a pause. The otter looked Ned up and down. "Well, I commend your gumption, indeed I do," he said finally. "It's dangerous work, there's no denying it. But what about those knights? That's what they were sent to do, wasn't it – kill the monster? Are you sure you want me to describe it to you? Might put you off, you know."

"AIN'T EVEN GOT A PLAN"

NED SAT DOWN AND
NODDED AT THE
OTTER TO BEGIN.
"Well, you'll need
courage, right enough," said
Otter, stroking his whiskers. "It's a fearsome
enemy – the biggest thing I've ever seen. The first
time it flew over I dived underwater, I have to
admit – that gigantic black shape coming over."

Tuff raised an eyebrow.

"And then there's this huge roar – a terrible
noise, deafening!"

"It sounds a very frightening monster," said
Ned.

"Indeed. It's just possible, perish the thought,

that what we're dealing with here is a d—"

"A what?" asked Piggy, looking up from his snack.

"Time enough to find out what it is when we get to where it lives," said Tuff rapidly, trying to catch the otter's eye.

Otter stopped. "It is a very large and very fierce beast – that's all I can say for sure," he finished.

Ned gazed into the water. "When does this monster come out?" he asked.

"Usually late afternoon or at dusk," said the otter. "Most days, that is. You sense him first, a huge shadow, and then there's this fearful roar. Most of the humans have left their houses, packed up, taken what they can, and gone."

"Oh dear, oh dear," said Dilly.

"Then there's this awful change everywhere," Otter went on, "as if the land's not ours now. With that shadow up there, the air no longer smells fresh. We're keeping our heads down and hoping for the best. Those knights were riding

along, flags waving, playing their pipes. Stupid!
Asking for trouble. Then the monster soared out,
roaring. I took cover in the stream, but I heard
screams. When I finally thought it was safe to
come out, they'd all gone."

Ned shifted uneasily. Tuff's tail was between
his legs; Dilly's ears were laid back, and the
whites of her eyes showed. As for Piggy, he'd
found some nice mud to roll in.

"Ned dear," Dilly said finally, in her soft voice,
"I know you think it your duty and all, and of
course I'm with you there, but isn't this really
foolish? Shouldn't we go back to the palace?
Perhaps it's our duty to stay and look after the
king?"

Tuff said nothing. Eventually he muttered
contemptuously: "Dooty!" then added bitterly,
"And he ain't even got a plan!" He snorted and sat
with his back to the others.

Ned got up and walked over to a stunted alder;
he stood there, looking at the sky as the light

faded. Then he noticed that the bark of
the tree was flaking, and some of the
leaves looked scorched and shrivelled; the
earth around was parched. He felt in his
pocket for the golden ball.

As the animals watched Ned, Tuff
turned round again, suddenly anxious.

"A difficult decision," said Otter
respectfully.

Ned turned and walked back to them.
"Friends," he said, "I've decided I must go
on. But I go alone."

The animals stared at him. Then they
all started talking at once:

"Never think it, dear, never think it! I
couldn't let you go on your own . . ."

"I'd certainly advise against that, Mr
Ned! Not something to tackle alone.
Perhaps . . ."

Tuff started running around Ned.
"Stupid boy – always said he was stupid, and

I dare say I always will," he yapped. "How he could manage on his own beats me! What have you ever done, Ned, but you haven't messed up, eh? No wonder they call you Butterfingers!"

"Don't call me Butterfingers," said Ned.

"Well, you can't even carry a bucket of water across the yard without spilling it!" barked Tuff. "It's no wonder the stable master shouts at you, you lumping great fool! Trip over your own shadow, you would. No wonder the cook shoos you out of the kitchen whenever she sees you. Why, you've only got to look at eggs to make them crack. You've only got to—"

"All right, all right, Tuff—" started Ned, raising a hand as if to calm him down.

"If you think I'm letting a great lummox like you set out on your own, you're very much mistaken, my boy! I've got my dooty too, you know – it's not just you that waffles on about dooty—"

"Enough, enough! I accept!"

"Accept?"

"I accept your help," said Ned, smiling. "I couldn't do it without you, really I couldn't, Tuff. I'd be lost without you."

Tuff sat down. His gruff voice softened. "Indeed you would, indeed you would." His small stump of a tail began to wag and he grinned up at them all.

But as they settled down to sleep that night, pressed close to the trees, Dilly shivered at the thought of what lay ahead. And she wondered, in the deepest part of her heart, if she was up to the challenge that lay before them. As for Ned, though he lay close to her as usual, and she heard his regular breathing, his eyes were wide open, staring into the darkness.

THE GREEN BOAT

"NOW," SAID THE OTTER THE NEXT MORNING. "It's too dangerous to go over the bridge and along the road. But under the bridge there's a small boat. I suggest you go down river on that for a while. It's a bit of a detour, but safer because the trees line the banks and much of the river is shaded and under cover. It joins the road again further along."

"A boat?" asked Ned. "But will it take all of us – Dilly as well?"

"Bit of a tight squeeze, but it should be all right."

"I'm not sure I like the sound of a boat, Ned dear," said Dilly.

"Come on, Dilly. It'll be safer. All right with you, Piggy?"

Piggy snorted. "Give it a go, give it a go."

"I'll accompany you, if I may," said Otter. "I can swim alongside. I think I'd like to do my bit in this adventure and help with monster-slaying."

"I can't ask you to put yourself in any danger for us," Ned said.

Otter waved a paw dismissively. "You need me," he told him. "No one knows the river like me."

"Then we'd be glad to have you," said Ned.

Tuff grinned. This was more like it – a few more sensible friends and they might even come up with a plan! "Why, we're getting to be almost a little army – the princess's army, so to speak! That measly old monster will take one look at us and turn to jelly. Come on – let's go get the monster!"

Otter led them to the small red-brick bridge; it curved low over the water, casting its dark shadow in reflection. He ran down the bank and

Ned scrambled after him. Hidden under the
foot of the bridge was a long, shallow boat with a
punting pole; it had once been bright green, but
now most of the paint had flaked off and it looked
uncared for. It rocked violently as Ned got in.

"Come on, Dilly. Come on, Tuff and Piggy.
Careful now!"

He stood steadying the boat and held out
his hand to help Dilly. On shaking hooves she
made her way down the sloping bank. The boat
wobbled precariously as she stepped in
and she gave a nervous whinny.

"Steady, steady!" said Ned.

Then Tuff jumped in and sat jauntily at the prow. Piggy, frowning, followed, taking a big leap and landing near Ned. The boat rocked wildly.

"Cor! This is an adventure and no mistake!" said Piggy. "Thought my days were marked out by grub and mud. Never thought I'd be off down a river with members of the court!"

"Time to get this straight, Piggy," said Ned. "We are not members of the court, whatever you were led to believe. We work in the palace stables. Do you still want to come?"

There was a pause. Tuff gave a little growl and turned his back on Ned, but Piggy grinned. "Oh well," he said. "Close to the court, so to speak. Close enough. And it is an adventure. Be glad when it's lunch time, though!"

Otter dived into the water beside them. Ned pushed off with the pole, and the boat, with its strange assortment of passengers, slid quietly off. The river veered away from the road, as Otter had said it would, and curved around in a long loop, almost turning back on itself.

Otter swam alongside the boat, his sleek brown head parting the water and making a neat V of ripples. Then, on the bank, Ned saw some old pear trees at the bottom of a neglected garden.

"Hang on," he said. "Free food!"

He drew in to the bank again, hopped out of the boat and picked several green pears. He stuffed them into his pockets and climbed back aboard. As he stretched over the side of the boat, he felt his jerkin catch against the wooden side,

94

and the golden ball popped out of his pocket and fell into the water with a splash!

"I've dropped the princess's ball!" cried Ned.

"Stupid boy!" barked Tuff. "Not called Butterfingers for nothing! Never known a boy like you for—"

"Will you be quiet, Tuff! Help me find it quickly!" He leaned over the side of the boat.

Piggy shuffled forward. "What's up?"

"Stupid boy has dropped the princess's ball," said Tuff. "Told him not to bring it with him, but oh no, he knew best. 'She'd want it, Tuff,' he said. 'It's her special ball.' Well, not so special that he goes and drops it!"

"Help me get it. I mustn't lose it!" said Ned.

But it was bobbing away, swept along in the current, further and further downstream. As they watched, it swung round in a little eddy towards the bank and disappeared among some reeds. Ned pushed the boat in the same direction. Dilly lurched unsteadily on her legs and whinnied.

"Can you see it, Otter?" Ned called.

Otter swam around, dived down and came up again, shaking his head.

Ned and Tuff peered over the edge of the boat. The water looked very dark and all they could see was their reflections staring back. Then the bushes on the bank rustled. As Ned glanced up, he caught a flash of reddish-brown between the overhanging branches, but then, almost immediately, it was gone. Drawing into the bank, he jumped out of the boat, beating back vegetation with his feet. Tuff and Piggy got out too and snuffled around the undergrowth.

The ball was nowhere to be found.

"What shall I do?" cried Ned. "I can't lose the princess's ball. She'll never forgive me!"

MOUSE

"STOP MOANING, BOY – NOTHING WE CAN DO ABOUT IT," SAID TUFF. "If you hadn't been so foolish, we wouldn't have had to waste time. Anyway, if that namby-pamby princess can only worry about—"

"She's not namby-pamby! She's the smartest—"

"Listen, boy! If that princess is only worried about a ball when we've come all this way to save her, then she's the most ungrateful little madam I've ever met."

"Will you stop talking like that about—?"

"He's right in a way, dear," said Dilly from the boat. "She'll be so grateful to be rescued that she won't even miss the ball."

"Do you think so, Dilly?"

"Of course, dear. Now, shouldn't we go on? We've looked and looked, but we've got more important things to do. The sooner we find this monster and save the princess, the better."

"Yes, yes, you're right. Thank you for looking."

They rejoined Dilly in the boat and set off, Ned still looking out for Bella's ball as they floated along. The river had started to curve back to the west again and soon ran alongside a cornfield, its ploughed furrows stretching away from them in stripes of browny-yellow.

"The road is just across there," said Otter. "The river passes through open fields here, and we might be seen. Best if we leave the boat under this willow and go through the corn. We can join the road on the other side."

They tied up the boat and got out. Dilly heaved a sigh of relief at being back on firm ground. Piggy looked hopeful and started to snuffle around for acorns. As they looked around, they saw that the ears of corn were withered; many lay flattened on the ground as if something huge and heavy had landed there. Above them, in the vast grey sky, they saw several black and white birds and heard the familiar cack-cack-cack.

"Uh-oh," said Dilly.

"They're far away," said Ned. Then, in the distance, he saw a plume of smoke!

Otter ran ahead to see what was going on; when he returned, he looked worried. "There's obviously been a bit of a fire," he told them. "Looks as if it's out now, but I'm not sure what caused it."

The smoke billowed about at the end of the field. The air was sultry and smelled of ash. Although it was hard to see the sun, it was very hot. Far ahead, the shadow-cloud loomed threateningly.

"We must hurry through the corn," said the otter.

So they made their way tiredly between the

rows of dying corn stalks. The magpies had
disappeared, but the smoke hovered over them,
smelling acrid and ominous. Dilly led the way,
with Ned on her back, trampling the corn
with her hooves. The dog, the pig and the otter
followed behind, half hidden by the stalks.

"Watch it!" came a little voice.

Dilly stopped suddenly and Ned almost fell
over her ears.

"That's my house you nearly trod on," said the
voice.

Ned got off, peered down between the rows
and saw a little field mouse balancing on an ear of
corn. "Hello," he said.

"Hello," said the
mouse. "I know it
doesn't look much,
but it's my home.
Don't want you lot
treading on it, do I?"

"I'm very sorry. We didn't see it."

"No one sees it," said the mouse sadly. "Took me ages to make my nest here, and no one notices. A master craftsman couldn't have done better, but it means nothing to passers-by. Tread on it without even looking, they will. Or plough it up. The times I've had to start all over again you wouldn't believe."

"It's a very nice house," said Ned politely. "I can see that now. Very sorry, I'm sure. We're on an urgent journey, you see."

"May I ask where you're off to?" asked the mouse.

"We're off to kill the monster."

"Oh, I'll be glad if someone deals with him. A right nuisance he is. Fair ruined this field with his dark cloud, blasts of fire and smoke. The far end of the field was singed when he flew over. I was worried it would all catch fire!"

"Fire . . ." pondered the otter. "Why, it sounds like a d—"

"Hush," said Tuff quickly.

"Have you seen him?" Ned asked the little mouse.

"Yes, like a great black shadow flying over, making this awful noise, and his great claws hanging down."

"Claws!" Dilly muttered.

"Don't you worry, Mouse, we'll get that old monster," said Tuff quickly.

"Jolly good thing. Get life back to normal," said the mouse.

"Yes, that's the reason for our journey. We're off—" started Ned.

"Monster-slaying!" cried Piggy and Tuff.

"And to rescue the princess," said Ned.

"Ooh, an adventure! Mind if I—"

"Tag along?" said Tuff.

"Yes," said the mouse.

"Hop aboard, Mouse," said Ned. "We'll be glad to have you."

The little mouse ran up Ned's sleeve and sat inside the collar of his jerkin, while Ned climbed back on Dilly and took the reins.

"Off we go! Off to do a bit of monster-slaying and save the princess!"

A DARK WOOD

THEY FOLLOWED THE NARROWING ROAD AS IT WOUND UPWARDS; AT LAST THEY SAW AHEAD OF THEM A SMALL WOOD, FULL OF DARK AND TWISTED TREES. It seemed to get hotter and hotter the further they travelled. Ned loosened his jerkin and took a deep breath. Would this journey ever end? As they approached the wood, he looked up at the crooked branches and just made out the shapes of some little birds huddled together in the gloom. It was hard to see the way ahead clearly; the branches curved overhead almost like a tunnel. Dilly took a few steps forward, then stopped.

"It's so dark, Ned," she said. "I'm not sure I want to go in there."

"It's the only way, Dilly," said Ned. "And besides, it's hard for anything overhead to see us – couldn't be better cover! Come on!"

He patted her flank. As she gave a sudden jump forward, he caught his head on a low branch and almost fell. He swung half out of the saddle, clinging on with one leg and one hand.

"Clumsy boy," said Tuff under his breath. "Needs watching every moment, that one."

Here and there, among the bracken, dead leaves and pine needles on the ground, Ned could just make out the gleam of little eyes. Occasionally he heard a rustle and saw the back legs of a rabbit dodge out of sight. A startled bird gave out a cry, but soon all was quiet again. Too quiet. Dilly laid back her ears.

Meanwhile Tuff and Piggy were having a great time – Piggy with the acorns he found as he snuffled about, and Tuff because there was an exciting smell of rabbits.

They walked in single file under the low

branches and slowly made their way past a
tangled ivy-covered bush.

"Why, hello," came a smooth voice from behind
the bush.

They all jumped. Dilly came to a sudden stop
and Ned almost fell off again.

"What have we here then? A little procession,
no less, of very, very interesting animals."

"Who's there?" said Tuff and
began to growl, low in his throat.

"Don't be alarmed, friends,
don't be alarmed," said
the voice. "Just interested,
you know, at such
a strange little
procession
through my wood."

From the shadow of the bushes emerged
the dull red fur and long tail of a fox. It was
a thin but rather handsome fox, with
one ear.

The otter slunk back quickly
and the mouse slipped
quietly down Ned's neck.

"Your wood? Didn't
know this wood belonged
to anyone," said Tuff.

Ned got down off Dilly's
back. "We want no trouble,

BUTTERFINGERS

and mean none," he said. "We're just passing through."

"Passing through to where, boy?" asked the fox in his low, slinky voice.

"Mr Ned to you, Foxy," said Tuff angrily.

"Mr Ned? Well, I didn't realize I was being honoured with Mr Ned," said the fox.

"Mr Ned from the court, I'll have you know, so you mind your ps and qs, Foxy!"

"From the court? Well, well, honoured indeed! You wouldn't think you were from the court to look at you, but then, one can never tell by appearances. Why, who would have thought such an odd little group would have been carrying treasure?"

"What treasure?" Ned quickly strode over to the fox, who casually extended a paw as if to fend him off.

"Ah, how impressive. So used to treasures that you can scatter them as you travel. Must be nice to have so many that you can lose one or two if you like."

108

"What are you on about, Fox? Have you found anything of ours?"

The fox grinned a wide grin. His teeth looked large and yellow. Then, from behind his back, he produced the golden ball and tossed it up and down.

"Give me that!" yelled Ned. "That's the Princess Bella's ball and I'm taking it to her."

Tuff started to growl again. "Hand it over, you villain," he said.

"Villain? Oh, charming! Catch!" Fox called to Ned, and he threw the golden ball to him. Ned grabbed for it and missed. It rolled along the ground and he ran after it.

"You stole it from us!" barked Tuff.

"Stole? Me? Never," said the fox, and he laughed a low laugh. "I found it where you foolishly dropped it. Oh, I've been following your progress for a while. Such an odd group of friends. May I ask, pray, where you are going?"

"Er . . . we are . . . like I said . . . just passing

through." Ned quickly put the ball safely back in his pocket.

"Oh," drawled the fox. "Just passing through, are you? Dropping golden balls as you go. A little group of people, from the court" – he smiled his wide smile – "almost a little army, no less, a little more ragged and less well equipped than the army of knights that came through some time back, but a little army nevertheless."

"I don't like your smile," said Tuff.

"Don't you? What a shame. And I so like your scowl." The fox slowly looked round at the rest of the group. "Are you on the same useless venture as those knights, pray?"

"Yes, we are," said Ned. "But we don't think it useless. We intend to do a bit of—"

"Monster-slaying!" came the tiny voice of the mouse.

"Ah." The fox scratched his one ear nonchalantly. "Monster-slaying? Well, well, well, well."

"Have you seen the monster?" asked Otter.

The fox came a little nearer. "Ah, well, to be honest," he told them, "I have seen the monster and I can't say I like it. For one thing, it tends to scorch my trees as it flies over."

"Your trees! Why—"

"Well, good luck to you, I say," grinned Foxy. "You'll need it."

"Well, we'll be on our way," said Ned. "Goodbye, Mr Fox."

"Actually, don't know if I might just tag along . . ." said the fox.

"What!" yapped Tuff.

"Tag along?" said Ned. Beside him, he heard Dilly give a little groan. "No need for that, no need at all," he went on. "We can manage."

"Think I will, all the same," said the fox. "You never know – I might come in useful. And I'd like to see a bit of monster-slaying, I can't deny it."

There was an uncomfortable pause. Then: "Very well," said Ned. "Do, er, tag along then."

"We're going monster-slaying!" chorused
the animals as they set out again, but rather
half-heartedly this time. They all felt slightly
uneasy about the fox and kept casting backward
glances at him as he sauntered along behind the
procession, his large white-tipped tail swinging.

A SONG

IT WAS HOT AND AIRLESS. They had been travelling for days and there still seemed so far to go. The food had run out. The sky was a strange yellow, and the river, which they had kept in sight for many a mile, dried up to little more than a shallow stream. Now the road was merely a dusty track which scored the earth, winding gradually upwards through the bare land. Apart from a few stunted trees and sparse bushes, there was no cover. And no sign that the knights had come this way. Perhaps, thought Ned, they hadn't made it this far.

"The open plain," said Foxy. "Take my advice, friends, and hurry across. I've had most of my scrapes, most of my fur-raising adventures, across the open plain."

With each step they took, they were saddened and troubled to see the devastation of the land. Far ahead, the shadow-cloud was larger and seemed to spread towards them, as if beckoning them on.

"There's no denying it, Ned, lad, I feel a bit down," said Tuff. "This here land, it don't seem like land as we know it – seems kind of foreign, like, kind of frightening, like. Got to be honest, lad, it makes me feel—"

"Me too, dear," said Dilly in a rush. "It's a terrible place we're coming to. Let's change our mind, dear; it's not too late."

"I'm hungry," said Piggy.

"You're not the only one, Piggy, old thing," said Tuff.

"And when I'm hungry, I get uneasy," added Piggy. "And I've been uneasy a long while."

"We're all together – not much harm can befall us if we're all together," said Ned.

"They know nothing, poor fools," said the fox with a smirk.

"Quiet, Foxy," said the otter. "If we're such fools, why are you with us?"

"Curious, just curious, dear thing. To see where you end up. And how you cope when you get there."

They carried on, following the dusty track towards the foothills of the high mountains; ahead, they could just make out the rounded shapes of a few sheep trying to graze amongst mounds of heather and gorse. As they approached, the sheep scuttled away.

When the friends sat down to rest, Dilly looked about her nervously and Tuff put his nose between his paws. "Ain't got much heart to go on, to tell the truth, lad," he said to Ned. "Ain't got much heart for courage and dooty!"

"What?" said Ned. "Why, you're the bravest dog I know. Don't say that, Tuff. Don't you lose heart, or I will too."

They sat in silence for a
while. Then Dilly raised her
head. "Do you hear what I
hear?" she said.

"Well," said Tuff, "don't that
put the heart straight back in a dog? Nuffing
more normal or pleasant sounding than that,
that's for sure."

Filling the air with piercing high notes came
the trilling song of a lark. Tuff stood up, his tail
wagging.

"How come such a small bird makes such a
loud song?" he said. "Always wondered that. A
song you can hear when the lark is too high even
to see."

"That's the best song in the world," said Ned.
"Can't be much wrong with the world if there's
still a sound like that, now can there?"

And as they looked up, listening to the lark's
song – the only sound in that silent stretch of
land – they saw a swift movement and the tiny

bird flew down and landed near a gorse bush.

"Well I never did!" said Tuff. "You're a sight for sore eyes and no mistake."

"Where you all off to?" the little bird asked, her head tipped to one side. She hopped nearer and perched on a twig. "Hope you know it gets dangerous further up. I usually see folks going in the other direction, not following that dark cloud. Except for those knights, that is."

"You've seen the knights?" asked Ned eagerly.

"Yes," replied the lark, shaking her head gravely. "But that was days ago and they haven't returned. No sign of them, no sign at all."

Ned's heart sank. "They're meant to be slaying the monster," he explained, "and rescuing the princess."

"We heard they were in trouble, Lark," said Tuff. "That's why we're here – on a sort of a quest, like; we're feeling bad about it, that's for sure."

"Worse by the minute," said Dilly softly.

"But we intend to go on and finish what we

came to do," said Ned solemnly.

The bird looked at them with her bright eyes, her head turning quickly from one to the other. "Brave or foolish," she said. "Perhaps both."

"But what of you, dear?" asked Dilly. "Why are you still here? It seems there is no one left in this part of the land – only some magpies, and we haven't even seen them for a while."

"There are still a few of us birds about," said the lark, "but most of the animals have gone from these parts. They're all afraid of the monster – with good reason. It swoops down and carries off anything it sees. Most birds have flown down river where it's safer, and where there's still some green. But me – well, it's my home, you see. My family have lived under this gorse bush for generations."

"It's not nice to have to leave your home," said Dilly, with feeling.

"Home's home, I say," said the lark. "I'll not be moved from my home." She hopped up and down on a branch and trilled even louder. "And if you can do anything about that fearful monster, why, we'll all be grateful."

"We'll do our best, that's for sure," said Ned.

"But how?" Tuff looked at them in despair.

"We're still hoping he'll come up with a plan—" started Otter.

"But that boy never thought of a plan in his life!" finished Tuff.

"We'll know when we get there," said Ned firmly. "What lies ahead, Lark?"

"The track follows the stream round two bends, then climbs the lower slopes of the hills. Behind them is a range of rocks and then tall craggy mountains, reaching to the sky. That strange shadow-cloud hovers over them. Those crags are dark and scary places. I don't go near."

"Oh, Ned dear . . ." started Dilly, but her voice faded as she looked at the boy's face.

The lark gave a little trill. "You're a brave boy," she said. "Brave and foolish. But good luck to you, sir. I might as well go a little of the way with you."

Ned looked at Lark. She tilted her head on one side and her bright eyes gleamed.

"Thank you," he said. "We'd love to have you with us."

Strange, how Ned started to feel a little braver with the tiny bird flying before him.

THE MOUNTAIN CRAG

NOW THE WAY BECAME HARDER AND HARDER, A STEADY UPHILL CLIMB. The dark cloud overhead was bigger than ever, but although the sun was almost invisible through the mist, it felt hotter than ever. They were all tired, hungry and anxious.

And then they came to a stretch of land that was even more bleak, more barren than before.

The thin yellow stream wound through sedge, clumps of burned grass and misshapen alders, their knotted, exposed roots barely clinging to the sloping earth. The parched track was strewn with boulders.

There was silence but for the sudden cack-cack of some magpies, high above them. They watched as four of the birds wheeled around and flew off in the opposite direction.

"It's been a long time since we saw them," said Ned. "Never thought I'd say this, but I've almost missed those wretched birds – they make life seem a little more normal."

"I don't like it," said Piggy. "Everything seems wrong, and I'm hungry."

"Keep together, men," said Otter. "Close ranks!"

Dilly picked her way along carefully and Ned held on tight. Tuff's ears were back and his tail down and he followed Dilly's hooves closely.

All through the latter part of the journey Ned had felt a growing heaviness and weary dread. Now, finally, Dilly slowed down until she stopped altogether. All the animals came to a halt behind her.

"Walk on, walk on, Dilly," whispered Ned in the pony's ear.

But Dilly's sturdy body did not move. Tuff sat down firmly and gave a little growl. They gazed up at the mountains.

"We must go on, Tuff," said Ned. "Come on, friends."

At the back, Foxy sat down and yawned. "Well, well, well, well," he said. "What a surprise. A touch of nerves?"

Ned frowned at him, then leaned forward again and spoke quietly in the pony's ear. "Dilly, we can't turn back. Don't let Foxy see we're scared."

Eventually Dilly consented to move off. The shadow-cloud now hovered right above them, dark and menacing. Ahead, rearing up like a giant, was a strange, black, pinnacled mountain crag, higher than all the surrounding peaks. Ned saw a puff of pale smoke waft out of a dark shadowed crevice near the top of the crag; it hovered for a moment like a small grey cloud before dissolving in the air.

Once more Dilly snorted and stopped. Her nostrils flared and her ears lay flat. All the animals behind halted again. There was another pale puff of smoke and a sudden acrid smell.

They huddled together, wondering what to do. Then, in front of Dilly's hooves, there was a sudden bob of fur and a flash of white tail! A rabbit hopped out, stopped for a second to stare, whiskers quivering, and then was gone. Quick as a flash, without thinking, Tuff rushed off in pursuit. The rabbit disappeared into a small hole near the base of the crag.

Immediately Ned jumped down and ran after the dog, grabbing his haunches just in time before he disappeared into the burrow.

"Ow! Get off me!" yapped Tuff's muffled voice from the hole.

"Tuff! I've told you before! No rabbits!" Ned tugged at Tuff's back legs and pulled him out. As he did so, he slipped on the earth and landed flat on his face. He sat up, trying to wipe off the mud, ignoring Tuff's scowl.

All the animals laughed, Foxy a lot longer than the rest. Dilly felt a little better. "Oh, look at you now, Ned dear," she said. "You can't save a princess looking like that. Wipe your face, dear."

Tuff continued to glare at Ned. "Nearly got that pesky rabbit till you stopped me!"

"Oh no you didn't!" came the rabbit's squeaky voice from inside the burrow. "Nah nah na-nah nah!"

Instinctively Tuff leaped up again.

"Tuff!" cried Ned desperately. "We are not here to chase rabbits!"

"Darn me! First bit of fun I've had on this awful journey, and you stop me!"

"Why are you acting like this?" said Ned, angry for once. "We've more important things to do!"

"Oh yeah? It's not as if we've got a plan!"

Ned screwed up his face in frustration. For the first time he raised his voice. "Stop going on about it! We'll think of a plan—"

"Don't quarrel! Please don't quarrel!" pleaded Dilly.

Suddenly, even as she spoke, from the mountain came another puff of smoke, bigger than before. And this time it was accompanied by a terrible roar; then a sheet of flame burst from the mountainside!

Ned nearly cried out. He clung to Dilly, who bucked and reared, while Tuff gave a piteous whine. As Ned craned his neck upwards, he saw something black begin to emerge from the crevice! There was another roar of flame, a billow of smoke and a fearful noise.

These were followed by the spikes of huge black wings, then a long scaly neck; short legs, the feet tipped in pointed claws. Then the neck curved round towards them. Ned gasped when he saw the huge head: there was a long snout with flaring nostrils which streamed with smoke, gleaming orange eyes and a gaping mouth, showing the most vicious-looking teeth. Finally the monster's huge body was visible, ending in a long pointed tail!

"Oh no!" cried Ned. He stared up in horror.

"It's ... it's . . .

a dragon!"

ALONE!

THE DRAGON'S HUGE WINGS SPREAD WIDE, CASTING A SHADOW ON THE GROUND. The beast hung as if suspended, its wings scarcely moving. Suddenly, arching its neck, it gave a roar so chilling and so harsh that Dilly kicked up her heels and whinnied in fright! Tuff started a furious barking.

Ned quickly clamped Tuff's jaws shut, but Dilly gave another terrified whinny. At this, the monster raised its wings and soared out of its cave.

The wind caused by the vast wings rustled in the scraggy bushes and half-dead trees. Ned's hair lifted and, despite the heat around him, his skin felt chilled and his body trembled.

Gazing fearfully upwards, he saw the dragon turn its head in their direction. The gigantic body twisted in the sky. With another horrific roar of flame, it started to glide down towards them!

"Flee, Tuff! Flee, Dilly! Flee, my friends."

There was a pause and then, in a mad rush, the animals fled. Mouse rushed down Ned's collar. The lark soared up into the sky and disappeared. Piggy gave a high-pitched squeal and his four trotters trotted as they never had before. The otter, and even the fox – all rushed off in terror.

Ned let go of Dilly's bridle and, for the first time in his life, he whacked her hard on her flank. "Flee, Dilly!"

Dilly reared up and galloped off down the hillside and into the bushes, whinnying as she went. Tuff's fur stood up on end, his ears pricked, his nose twitched. He gave a harsh bark and suddenly tore off into the bushes after her. It took all Ned's courage not to follow them. But he knew he must stay and find the princess. He pressed himself against the rock.

The monster hung for a moment in the sky, watching the animals run. Then it gave another terrible roar, tipped its wings, gathered speed and followed!

Ned's eyes scanned the hillside. He could no longer see his friends, only the dragon's diminishing form, head down, searching, searching . . . He watched and watched, praying for gentle, loyal Dilly and Tuff, his dearest friend, and for the other animals who had so courageously accompanied them on this foolish journey. He did not realize his eyes were wet. He did not realize his breath was coming in quick gasps. He was unaware of everything around him, his eyes fixed on the dragon.

Ned watched until his eyes were sore, but he did not see the dragon land; after a while the spiky black shape disappeared from view.

He sank down, exhausted.

132

Tuff and Dilly, his
two dearest friends,
were gone. Oh Tuff,
thought Ned. And we
quarrelled – oh, what if I never see you again? He
prayed that the dragon would never find them
and that they would somehow find their way back
to the palace grounds.

The palace. Home. It was like a dream, the
homely warmth of the stables, where he belonged,
with gentle Dilly in her stall and the grumpy
little dog next to her. But he was now alone in
this bleak, barren landscape.

Above him reared the black mountainside,
the jagged rock stretching up so high that Ned
could scarcely see the top. Fissures, cracks and
seams etched its surface like scratches on jet. The
blackness gleamed. Sharp edges jutted from the
sides.

Yet up there, somewhere, the Princess Bella
waited to be rescued. He was sure of it.

Ned got to his feet. He took a deep breath, squared his shoulders and laid his hands on the hard rock. "Up you go, Ned," he told himself.

He scrambled for a foothold and pulled himself up. He was used to climbing his favourite elm tree, but he had never experienced anything as sheer and high as this. For a long time he painfully clawed his way upwards. The fog swirled about him and the wind moaned. The ground below was very far away.

"Don't look down," he said to himself, but even this thought brought a wave of dizziness.

Ned stopped, gasping for breath. His feet slipped and searched and ached; his fingers throbbed with pain. His hands were twisted and frozen; they could not let go and they could not change position. He waited, and gradually he found he could move them; he shifted his weight and started his slow climb once more, hoping he would not be spotted by the dragon.

At last, at last, he neared the summit.

He paused, clinging like a martin to a wall. He
was no more than this; he was less than this, for
a martin could fly off and be free. He was a
dot, a minute speck made of pale colours —
faded brown leggings and oatmeal-
coloured jerkin and straw-like hair.
These were the only colours on
that vast black crag, hardly
visible, while all around
spread the endless grey
and black.

Then he raised
his head and
saw, near the
top, a gaping
dark hole.

The dragon's lair!

INSIDE THE DRAGON'S LAIR

NED HAD SCALED THE MOUNTAIN AND SCRAMBLED OVER THE LAST ROCK AND NOW HE LAY DOWN FOR A MOMENT, BREATHING HEAVILY. He was on a stony ledge at the entrance to a cave, high up on the mountainside. He glanced down and wished he hadn't. The ground, far below, seemed to tilt and fall away. The shadow-cloud lay around him in strands of black mist, touching him as if with long dark fingers. Ned shut his eyes, feeling dizzy.

Taking a deep breath, he looked into the dark hole of the dragon's cave. He was intensely aware that the dragon could return at any time. He shuddered as he remembered those terrible claws and teeth. Getting to his feet, he crept over to the entrance and tiptoed in.

There was a harsh smell of cinder and something else, something foul.

It was hard to see in the darkness, but gradually Ned's eyes made out the shape of the rock; the lair seemed to stretch on and on.

He heard a noise and, startled, pressed himself against the wall.

But it was nothing – perhaps the wind, perhaps an echo.

Ned's heart was thumping and his breath seemed loud. "Be brave, Ned," he said to himself. "Remember, be like a knight." He kept in his mind an image of the Princess Bella; it made him feel a little more courageous. Slowly he edged along the wall, feeling with his hands for the crevices and cracks as he went. The crevice narrowed and stretched back into further darkness.

If the dragon returned, he would be found. Found and eaten. A terrible fear gripped Ned. Supposing the princess had already become a meal for the dragon and he had come all this way in vain!

"It's no good worrying about such things," he said to himself. "I'll find out soon enough. Meanwhile, I must go on."

He crept further into the gloom. The rocky walls dripped with moisture and were horrid to touch. He felt terribly alone. Then, ahead, he saw a dim light.

As Ned made his way forward, he realized that the passage opened out into a long cave. His eyes widened. There, on the floor of this cave room in the middle of the mountain, was a rich purple Turkish carpet; hanging from the ceiling, an ornate gold lantern shed its flickering light in the dimness. Unlit torches lined the walls, and Ned saw that these followed the passage beyond the cave, deeper into the mountain. He could make out the intricate patterns on the carpet, bright with rich reds, blues and purples, yet stained with dark blotches. The light from the lantern cast strange shadows on the uneven walls. Ned's own shadow appeared huge, a strange, half-bent, creeping silhouette which exaggerated his gangly form, his spiky hair and his tensed shoulders. His shadow bent and rippled across the ridges of the rock and seemed to splinter into creases and cracks.

As Ned looked closer, he suddenly realized that the spattered stains on the carpet could only be (and here he could not suppress a shudder) the remains of the dragon's meal. He now made out several bones, bits of gristle and odd remnants of fur and feather. The carpet was stained with blood and the stench of old flesh filled the musty air.

Ned shivered, and his shadow shivered too, vast and quivering on the cave walls. He felt very vulnerable, standing there in the middle of that room.

Then, in the distance, he heard a roar! The dragon was returning!

But before he could panic, he felt something moving at his neck. It was Mouse. In his fear and exertion he had forgotten her. "Oh, Mouse," he whispered, but the little creature scampered under his jerkin and down his trousers, and darted across the carpet to disappear into a

Ned's head swivelled round after her. The crevice was little more than a crack in the rock, yet it looked almost wide enough for a skinny boy. Mouse had shown him a hiding place. Could he reach it in time? He heard his heart thumping in his chest.

He ran swiftly across the Turkish carpet, across the bones and the mess, across the great divide of the room, with his shadow leaping ahead of him as he went.

Suddenly there was a rush of wind and smoke! His heart lurched and he gasped. The dragon was back and an ear-splitting roar filled the cave!

Ned froze. Then he came to his senses and squeezed into the crevice.

Just in time, Ned! Just in the nick of time!

For smoke billowed into the cave, and heat and noise filled the space. Then the huge scaly body of the dragon entered. Magically, all the torches on the walls lit up!

Ned saw the huge beast in every fearful

detail: the glittering black scales, the red, gaping, many-toothed mouth. In one cruel claw dangled a sheep; in the other was a golden goblet. The dragon closed its wings and dropped the sheep and the goblet on the floor. The sheep bleated piteously and scuttled across the carpet. With a harsh laugh, the dragon sent out a tongue of flame, which hit the sheep like a whip. Ned shut his eyes in horror. When he opened them again, the sheep was dead!

BONES!

AS NED CROUCHED, HIDDEN FROM VIEW, HE SAW THE DRAGON TEAR AT THE FLESH OF THE SHEEP IT HAD KILLED. Chewing, chopping, grinding, burping, the dragon enjoyed its meal.

At last, with a loud belch and a puff of smoke, it was finished. There was a horrid mess left on the floor: bits of bone, hooves and other indigestible parts of the poor sheep. The dragon gave a huge yawn, opening its jaws wide and dribbling a little as it did so.

But instead of going to sleep, it moved out onto the rocky ledge, reared up and opened its wings. With a huge roar and a blast of smoke, it took off into the air. Immediately the torches along the walls went out.

Ned looked around for Mouse but she was nowhere to be seen. He really was totally alone now. But he took his courage in both hands, left the crevice and started to creep over to the passage that led from the far end of the cave. Without the torches, the further he went from the lantern, the darker it got. He had lost track of how long he had been in the cave, for day and night had no meaning here. He felt like a mole, or a worm that finds its way blindly, in the dark earth. All Ned could do was carry on, though a heavy dread sat in his heart. Cautiously, peering ahead in the gloom, he felt his way forwards.

It was not far and yet it seemed so. At last a little glow of light could be seen ahead. Ned quickened his pace. Suddenly his feet bumped against something;

something that gave way with a rattle. His heart missed a beat, but then he bent down and felt something hard, which seemed to crumble at his touch.

Ned drew back his hand in horror, his chest heaving in panic! He had touched a dead man! A dead man, still dressed in armour! His eyes gradually made sense of the shapes. There, lying crookedly across the floor as if thrown down, lay the skeleton of a knight!

Ned wanted to run back, but he made himself be calm. Eventually he felt able to look closer and saw that the bones had been picked clean. A plumed helmet sat atop a white skull, the teeth grinning mirthlessly. From under the helmet flowed long dark locks of hair; silver gauntlets covered the arm bones; and the still dimly shining breastplate lay over empty ribs.

His stomach lurching, the boy put out his hand and traced the engraving on the breastplate: a prancing lion, still showing a faint red tinge. This was the skeleton of Sir Pevner! The knight had made it all the way into the mountain to rescue the princess, yet had been killed! All that was left of him was a pile of bones and a few pieces of armour.

Sir Pevner, the king's champion, bravest of all the knights, had failed to destroy the dragon. The terrible monster had killed him and Ned couldn't help thinking that it could only be a matter of time before he became the dragon's next meal!

He mustn't think of that. He must only think of the Princess Bella. Ned looked down at poor Sir Pevner's skeleton. "No giving up yet, Ned," he said to himself. "It's up to you now. You came all this way to find Bella, and find her you will!"

The boy carried on towards the light. The passage curved round before opening out again into another cave. Cautiously, he peered in.

This cave was a little brighter, lit this time by rounded orbs of light coming from a golden candelabra suspended from the centre of the roof. There were unlit torches around the walls of the cave, which were hung with crimson drapes. Pieces of furniture were tipped over, as if thrown into the room, and another Turkish carpet lay on the rocky floor, this one clean and bright, covered with a scattering of gold coins and shiny beads. A large gilt mirror stood propped up near a wall and Ned tiptoed in and hid behind it. He peeped round . . .

And gave a silent gasp at what he saw.

THE GOLDEN TREASURE CHAMBER

THERE WAS A HUGE PILE OF TREASURE, LYING ALL HIGGLEDY-PIGGLEDY, ONE THING BALANCED UPON ANOTHER, REACHING UP NEARLY TO THE CEILING. There were half-open chests full of coins; there were rolls of silks and satins; there were strings of jewels, necklaces and crowns. There were golden goblets and paintings in gilded frames; there were the heads or arms of bronze and marble statues poking through a muddle of shiny objects; there were pieces of glittering armour, large gold chains of office, leather-bound books – Ned could hardly believe his eyes: all this splendour mixed up

together, one precious thing on top of another,
in a heap within the dark mountain!

The pile of treasure seemed to give out a light of its own, a golden gleam shining like a flame within the rocky cave. Ned stared and stared; then he craned his head and looked up. There, balanced precariously on the very top, was a small gilt chair, and on this chair sat the Princess Bella!

Ned's heart lurched. She was alive! She looked just the same: bright, shining, golden-haired, attired in the white dress she had been wearing on that wonderful – terrible – morning of her birthday. She was staring into space, a lost, empty look on her small perfect face.

Ned crept out from behind the mirror into that glowing place; all the goblets and bowls shone in the light of the candelabra, and in each winking gold or silver surface a tiny reflection of a princess glittered. There were hundreds of tiny princesses, in hundreds of tiny glittering mirrors, and each gave off light, as the princess

150

herself gave off light. How strange it was, Ned thought, to see such light inside such darkness; to see the princess sitting high up on the top of a sort of mountain – inside a mountain.

Then Ned saw her bend her head to her hands and heard the sound of sobs.

He quickly stepped forward. "Don't cry, Princess," he said. "I am here to save you."

The princess's head came up in a flash. She stared at Ned, one tear slowly rolling down her cheek. She wiped her eyes and looked at him, astonished.

"You! Ned the stableboy, Ned of the violets! How did you get here?" she whispered.

She leaned forward, looking down on him. Ned noticed that her hand was tied at the wrist by a long, loose green cord attached to an iron ring in the ceiling of the cave.

"Oh, thank goodness," she said, still whispering. "But I can hardly believe it's you. I've been expecting a knight to save me!"

Ned hung his head. This wasn't going quite the way he had intended.

"Oh," she whispered, seeing his face. "I didn't mean it like that. I've never been so pleased to see anyone. But, oh, Ned, whatever can you do to help me?"

"Lots of things," he said. "Why, I've come to defeat the dragon and take you back to the palace!"

"Ssh!" said the princess, looking anxiously at the cave entrance. "If you've come to save me, you'd better hurry up. It's very nice to see you, I'm sure, but—"

She stopped. Her eyes widened as they swept over Ned's odd assortment of armour. A curious expression came over her face.

"Ah well," she said at last, "an attempt at being a knight at least, if not quite what I had in mind. What I did have in mind were my father's knights, in shining armour – but they are all gone, all killed by the dragon, or they ran away in fear.

Oh, Ned, I heard them ride up and challenge the dragon. But it soared out and turned its fire on them. I heard the horses gallop off, if they were lucky. Otherwise they were eaten."

Ned gulped.

"So much for knights," Bella went on with a little grimace. "I thought that's what they were supposed to do – kill dragons! How you got here is a mystery to me. I know you, Ned. I've heard what they call you: Clumsy Ned. Butterfingers." Ned blushed. "And yet here you are. It's a kind of miracle."

She sat up straight in her chair and looked directly at him. "Well? What will you do? Do you have a plan?"

"Um . . . something will turn up, I'm sure," said Ned quickly. "When will the dragon return?"

"I don't know. It's probably gone to find more treasure, though if this pile gets any bigger it'll all fall down. The dragon won't let me go. Why it keeps me here I'll never know. Perhaps I'm part of its treasure. No, I'll never escape. Besides, I'm tied by this magic cord. You'll have to kill the dragon. And please be quick."

Ned moved a little closer and looked up at Princess Bella. He took in her forget-me-not blue eyes, her golden hair and her rose-coloured lips. Suddenly killing a dragon seemed an easy thing. Now that he had found Bella, he felt as brave as any knight.

THE ECHO

BELLA DREW HERSELF UP
AND LOOKED HER MOST
PRINCESSY.

"And how will you kill it? Do
you have a weapon?" she asked,
suddenly imperious. "Or merely
a bunch of violets to give it?"

"Oh, I have . . . this little
knife."

She tossed her head.
"Useless!" she said. "Do you have
any proper armour?"

"Just these bits . . . and pieces,"
said Ned, rather shame-faced.

"Oh, Ned!" she said,

exasperated. "Do you have anything
with which to kill a dragon
and save me? Which is
presumably why you came?
Do you have anything?"

Ned sighed; he felt sad
and hopeless. He put his
hands in his pockets and
shrugged.

Then he smiled. "I
brought this," he said. From
his pocket he took the golden ball
and threw it up to the princess. She caught it and
stared.

"What on earth do you think I can do with
this?"

Ned gulped. "Play with it?"

"Play with it?"

All of a sudden, as the princess raised her voice,
the whole cave – indeed, it seemed, the whole
mountain – was filled with an echo!

Play with it . . . Play with it . . .
with it . . . with it . . .

"It's your special treasure . . ." cried Ned in a rush.

Treasure . . . treasure . . . sure . . . ure . . . went the echo.

"Don't shout!" whispered the princess. "There's this terrible echo. That's why I've been trying to whisper. Keep your voice down."

"It's your special treasure," hissed Ned.

"Don't talk to me of treasure," she said, in a strange, high voice. "I've had enough of treasure; it's dragons who love treasure. I'm treasure; all this around me is treasure! My father, my palace, my garden, my liberty – those are my special treasures, not . . . not a – a ball!" She couldn't help but raise her voice in indignation.

Ball . . . ball . . . ball . . . lll . . . went the echo.

Ned sat down on the hard floor. He felt ashamed. "Sorry," he mumbled. "Perhaps when the dragon sleeps, we can creep past it and climb down the mountain and escape."

Bella gave a little shake of her shoulders. "I'm tied by this magic rope, boy. Can't you see? Really!" She gave a great sigh of impatience. "It can't be cut and it can't be untied." She leaned back in her chair and closed her eyes as if suddenly very tired.

Ned stood up. Bella opened her eyes. They looked at each other quietly.

"Then, Princess," he said finally, "I must kill the dragon."

"Oh, Ned," Bella whispered. "The knights came in an army and yet could not defeat the dragon. You are all on your own!"

"I came with an army!" said Ned.

"You did? Where is it?" she asked excitedly.

"Well – there were three of us to begin with – me, my dog Tuff and Dilly the pony. Then, after a bit, some other animals joined us—"

"Animals?" said the princess.

"A pig, and um . . . an . . . an otter . . . um . . . and a mouse . . . and . . ."

The princess stared at him.

"Um, and . . . a lark . . ."

The princess continued staring.

"And a fox! We all came to save you!"

"Oh, I see, yes," said Bella. "That'll help. Nothing like a few farmyard friends to sort out dragons. Nothing like the power and might of an old pony and a dog, a pig, an otter and a mouse! And what was it? A lark! And a fox? Just the thing. Well done! Don't know why you didn't bring a couple of chickens and a goat!"

Ned couldn't help it, he really couldn't. "I don't know why we bothered, Miss Snarky-pants!" he snapped.

Princess Bella gasped! Then suddenly she laughed. The laugh escaped her in a sweet sound and she looked surprised, as if a laugh was the most unexpected thing in the world. It echoed round and round the cave. It was a good sound to hear.

"We came together, my lady," said Ned, a little ashamed of his outburst now. "I'm . . . well, worried, you see. Because all these animals took fright when the dragon flew out, and they ran away," said Ned. "I told them to go," he added quickly. "They might have been eaten otherwise. Well – that left just me."

"Oh, Ned—" the princess started sadly.

"I don't know what has happened to them," continued Ned. "Dilly, my pony, and my dog Tuff – why, they've been with me since . . ." He gulped and couldn't go on.

There was a silence while the princess observed the golden ball in her lap. She started to toss it, idly, from hand to hand, the loose green cord moving with her as she did so. Then, with a little flick, she suddenly threw it up into the air. It flashed gold against the darkness of the rocky ceiling, and fell back into her hands. And with the movement, her heart lightened. She looked at Ned and, with a quick, surprising smile, threw the ball down to him.

"Catch!" she whispered.

He tried to catch it, but it bounced against his thumb and he dropped it. It rolled along the floor and he ran to pick it up.

"Butterfingers," said the princess. Ned hung his head, but when he looked up again, he saw on her face a soft, tender smile.

"You must keep hidden," she said softly. "Don't let it find you. Please, please, dear Ned, don't let the dragon find you."

Ned turned to go back down the passage. Suddenly he felt courageous and full of strength.

"Where are you going?" Bella cried anxiously. "Don't leave me!" And the echo rose up: Leave me . . . leave me . . . me.

"Leave you?" said Ned, remembering to whisper. "I could never leave you. But I intend to save you! I am going to get a sword!"

A SWORD

NED KNEW WHERE TO FIND A SWORD. He went swiftly back along the darkening passage until he came to the skeleton of Sir Pevner. He shivered anew as he saw it lying crookedly on the floor.

Half under the skeleton lay Sir Pevner's shield. Ned bent down and grasped the edge of it. As he pulled, the bones gave way, knocking against the breastplate with hollow sounds which echoed up the passage. Ned shuddered. He stood up clutching the shield, slipped his arm into the straps and held it in front of him.

He looked down at the skeleton again: in the

still-clenched gauntlet he saw
what he was searching for – the
silver sword. He prised it from
the knight's fist, then grasped
the hilt and held it aloft. As the
long blade flashed in the dimness,
he made out on its surface the
engraving of a lion.

Thus armed, Ned – beginning
to feel a little more like a knight–
went back up the passage to the
Princess Bella.

She watched him as he
approached. He still wore his
odd assortment of armour – a
bent breastplate, a knee protector,
an elbow protector and a gauntlet.
But he didn't look funny any
longer. The large shield and
sword of a champion knight
gleamed in front of him.

164

"Now, Princess," Ned began, "I think I've got a plan—"

But as he spoke, he heard a terrible roar! The very mountain seemed to shake. The dragon was returning and already Ned could feel the wind and smoke travel up the passage as the monster alighted on the outer ledge. Suddenly all the torches flared up on the walls.

As the roar started to die down, Bella whispered urgently: "Hide, Ned! The dragon will come in here!"

But as he started to move, he heard another sound – a familiar sound which made his heart leap. It was the high-pitched whinny of a frightened horse!

Ned didn't stop to think. He'd have known that whinny anywhere. It was his beloved Dilly! He ran back down towards the main cave and saw the dragon bend its neck and drop the pony from its mouth. Dilly careered across the cave in terror. The light from the torches lit her white rolling eyes as she galloped.

Ned ran towards her and saw the dragon opening its mouth to emit its fire! "Dilly!" he cried, and she reared up and stopped at his voice. "Up here – come through here!" And the echo of his voice reverberated through the cave. But Dilly seemed paralysed with fear.

The dragon stopped and stared. A boy! A skinny boy, holding in his arm a long silver sword! Smoke started to stream out of its nostrils.

Ned grabbed Dilly's bridle and ran helter-skelter up the passage to the treasure room. A long tongue of flame followed them. It licked the

walls of the cave, but Ned and Dilly were too quick, too quick! While they felt the great heat at their backs, they outran it.

A roar reverberated along the passage as the dragon followed. Before Ned could begin to think, the huge head came through the entrance to the cave. They stared into glowing orange eyes and grinning jaws. The dragon showed surprise and also something else – something like pleasure.

The torches flickered, the treasure glowed, and on top of the treasure, a beautiful princess sat leaning forward, her hand tied to the ceiling. At

the foot of the pile the dragon saw a stunned
pony – dinner – and a skinny boy – seconds! It
was not used to its victims running this far, but
it was more of a challenge.

The dragon bent over Ned and Dilly. Then, at the first flickering of flame, Bella's voice rang out!

"Catch!" (Catch! . . . Catch . . . catch . . . atch . . . ch . . . went the echo.)

The dragon stopped and slowly turned its head to look at her. Suddenly Bella's ball came winging through the air with a sure throw. Through the air it spun, shining, sparkling, spinning – the golden ball! Treasure!

Ned, in the blink of an eye, without a thought, dropped his sword, put out a hand and, for once, caught the ball!

The dragon's eyes narrowed and it paused. Food – or treasure?

ANIMAL ARMY

NED TOSSED THE BALL BACK TO BELLA. It flew high, its brilliant gold shining in the torchlight. Now the dragon's head moved back and forth, like a tennis spectator, watching the arcing ball. It seemed mesmerized, greedy for the treasure. To and fro between Ned and Bella went the ball. All time seemed to stop.

Bella caught a small movement out of the corner of her eye: something small was scuttling across the floor. It was a mouse! Back and forth Bella and Ned continued to toss the ball. Back and forth went the dragon's head as it followed the game with its eyes. Meanwhile, along the rock

walls animals crept in, one, two . . . three . . .
more! Bella made out an otter, a fox, a bird . . .
yet still her hand went up again and again,
catching the ball confidently, and all the while,
to her astonishment, she noticed more animals
creeping in. Hundreds of eyes gleamed in the
torchlight! They too swivelled back and forth as
they followed the track of the ball.

At first Ned was unaware of all the animals
coming into the cave to save them – not only the
"princess's army", but all the animals' friends and
relations; the whole animal kingdom, it seemed –
a real animal army, bravely entering the dragon's
lair to help the boy.

At the front, nearest to Ned, was Tuff. His
nose followed the progress of the ball just as the
dragon's did. His furry face was frowning in
concentration just as Ned's was. The dog looked
at Dilly, quaking by the treasure pile. He was so
worried for poor Dilly, and for his boy, that he
just couldn't help himself:

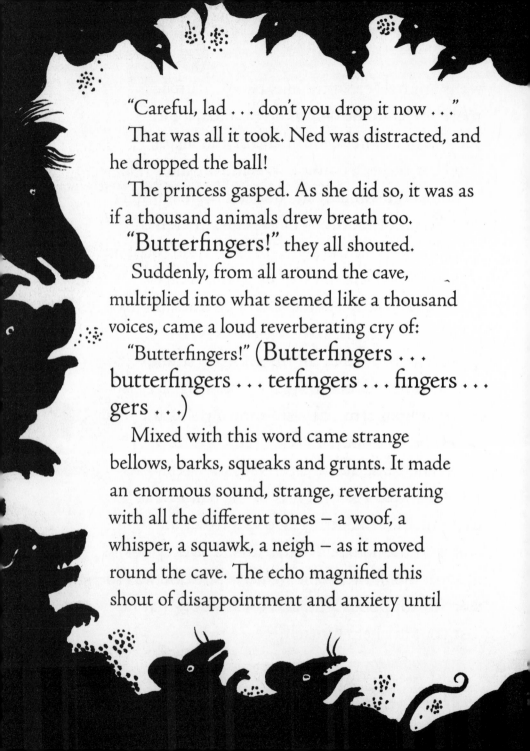

"Careful, lad . . . don't you drop it now . . ."

That was all it took. Ned was distracted, and he dropped the ball!

The princess gasped. As she did so, it was as if a thousand animals drew breath too.

"Butterfingers!" they all shouted.

Suddenly, from all around the cave, multiplied into what seemed like a thousand voices, came a loud reverberating cry of:

"Butterfingers!" (Butterfingers . . . butterfingers . . . terfingers . . . fingers . . . gers . . .)

Mixed with this word came strange bellows, barks, squeaks and grunts. It made an enormous sound, strange, reverberating with all the different tones — a woof, a whisper, a squawk, a neigh — as it moved round the cave. The echo magnified this shout of disappointment and anxiety until it seemed as if the mountain was alive with every animal in the kingdom, all calling out "Butterfingers!"

The dragon paused, unsettled by this huge cacophony of sound. The ball landed on the ground and rolled away.

A strange scene was being enacted there in the dark rocky chamber: a frightened boy standing frozen, his sword useless on the floor; a mighty but confused dragon; and a loud echo of different sounds vibrating around them. Then, from the hidden corners of the mountain, a group of animals moved forward, tense and ready for action – an otter, a pig, a rabbit, a bird, a fox! Then, to Ned's surprise, more rabbits, badgers, mice, rats, voles and shrews stepped out of the gloom. Birds of many kinds fluttered in the air – the cave seemed alive with all kinds of creatures!

If Ned was frozen for a second, staring at them, so too, for a moment, was the dragon. Its head was raised at the appalling sound and sight of the strange collection of animals coming out of the rock! Then, as if in slow motion, it seemed to gather its senses and bent over to release its fire at Dilly.

At this, Tuff rushed in front of her, barking at the top of his voice, and hundreds of yaps echoed around the room.

"You pesky dragon!" barked Tuff. "You keep away from my Dilly!"

The dragon slowly curved its head down to face the little dog.

"Just a mo, dragon old thing," came an unlikely voice.

The dragon stopped again.

There, next to Tuff, was the jaunty fox, and he was tossing Bella's golden ball up and down. Up it went, catching the light with its shining gold.

The dragon's eyes narrowed with greed.

"Now you see it," said Foxy, in a careless tone;
"now you don't." The ball disappeared somewhere
in his red fur. "Here's your treasure, Dragon.
Take it." The ball reappeared. "Whoops! Now
it's gone again. Irritating little object, isn't it? Oh,
here it is again!"

The dragon was transfixed and astonished. The
ball disappeared and reappeared like Foxy's smile.

Tuff grinned. "Hey-ho, Foxy, me old mate," he
said. "Always said you were to be depended on.
Pass it here, pal."

Foxy grinned and tossed the ball to Tuff, who
stopped it with his nose. He sped between the
legs of the dragon, dribbling the ball around
its scaly feet. It was the second time that this
irritating, tiny dog had incensed the dragon.
Smoke began to stream once more from its
nostrils.

But Tuff was away, twisting in and out, the
ball spinning and rolling. And now Piggy and
Otter, with all his friends, came running to

join in! Beneath the dragon the ball zipped
about from one animal to another. Lark flew
overhead near the dragon's snout. She led all
the other birds as they swooped in, aiming with
their pointed beaks. Rabbits, rats and little mice
scuttled up the dragon's legs, swarming over its
back to reach its head, nipping its ears and eyelids.
Otters leaped on the dragon's long pointed tail,
biting it as it lashed about.

The dragon was confused to see these small
creatures hanging from every limb, biting and
scratching. As Tuff, Piggy and Foxy sped under
and around the dragon, it reared up on its hind
legs, then lifted a foot and set it down

right on top of the rolling ball. Losing its balance, the dragon began to topple over.

In a blur of legs, tails and wings, the animals scurried aside or leaped off the falling dragon.

Ned's eyes took in flashes of a huge foot, two black wings, a rearing neck; then, momentarily, the princess, hands raised to her mouth in horror; the animals

darting away; and, above all this, heat and fire and panic!

It was a moment like no other. In one continuous movement, the ball rolled out from under the dragon and, quick as a flash, Tuff tossed it up to Bella. She put out one hand and caught it.

"Quick, Ned, the sword!" she cried.

Ned seized his sword and shield. As the dragon toppled over, it opened its mouth wide and let out a huge blast of fire, and Ned raised the large shield: the flame leaped around the metal, but the boy was unhurt. Then the beast crashed heavily to the ground, jaws gaping, and Bella threw the ball; it spun down through the air in an arc and landed right in the dragon's mouth!

"Goal!" yelled Tuff.

(Goal, goal, goal, goa . . .)

The dragon, struggling on the ground, coughed and choked.

At that instant Dilly galloped forward and

Ned leaped on her back, his assortment of armour gleaming, his large shield before him and his silver sword held high. He looked the very picture of a valiant knight!

"Go, boy!" barked Tuff.

Dilly, suddenly clear-headed, cried: "It's now or never!"

Letting out a battle cry, Ned charged with the sword. With the extra speed and force provided by Dilly, the sword plunged into the soft underbelly of the choking dragon and found its mark!

LANDSLIDE

THE DRAGON'S HEAD WAS STRETCHED UPWARDS, ITS EYES BLINKING IN DISBELIEF AND PAIN. It lay on its side where it had fallen, the ball still wedged in its great mouth. The sword stuck out from its yellow underside, and now a thin trickle of green liquid oozed down its belly. Its large legs shuddered and twitched. Still its head was raised, and its big orange eyes stared at Ned. Ned got down off Dilly's back and looked at the dragon's terrible face. Smoke began to stream from its nostrils, and then its long neck began to sway.

"Look out, Ned!" cried the princess, watching

from the top of the treasure pile.

As Ned backed away, the dragon's neck suddenly bent and juddered. The huge scaly head fell to the ground with a loud thud and the golden ball rolled out of its mouth. Smoke billowed out of the nostrils, but no flame came. All the friends stared transfixed. The huge eyes slowly closed; then the dragon's breath stopped. A little cloud of grey smoke hung in the air and then dispersed. There was silence.

Very cautiously, Ned approached. Then Tuff trotted up next to him and together they looked at the vast body of the dragon as it lay on the floor, wings folded crookedly, black and heavy on the Turkish carpet. It seemed to fill most of the chamber.

After a moment Tuff found his voice. "I . . . I reckon you did it, Ned. I reckon you did just what you set out to do, lad! Kill the old dragon. By crikey, you did it!"

"Is it really dead? Are you sure, Ned dear?" Dilly came up behind Ned and nuzzled him.

"Looks like it, Dilly."

One by one the animals approached.

"Well, well, never thought the boy had it in him. Most entertaining," said Foxy.

Ned looked at him. "I could never have done it without you, Foxy." Foxy grinned and gave a little half-bow. "And I could never, never have done it without you, Tuff. Or you, Dilly. I could never, never have done it without all of you!" He looked round at them. "How did you all get in here?" he asked. "You gave me the shock of my life when you all started yelling."

"Fair shook up the dragon, too," said Tuff. "That huge echo and all. And he couldn't believe his eyes when he saw us all. Nearly laughed, I did, but I was too busy at the time."

"Mouse came and found us and Rabbit showed us the way in," said the otter. "There was a tunnel near Rabbit's home."

"Never thought I'd be going down a rabbit's burrow," said Foxy in his slow voice, grinning as usual. "Always wanted to, of course."

The rabbit moved away, and all his relations hopped back nervously. Rabbit knew this fox was on his best behaviour, under the circumstances, but well – it wouldn't do to change the habits of a lifetime.

"I thought I'd lost you all," said Ned, looking around.

"You never lose your real friends, boy," said

Tuff. Then, suddenly, the dog gave a little yap and started to leap in the air. "Hooray!" he barked. The echo of that word went round and round the cave, and for once they delighted in the sound.

They grinned at each other. "Hooray!" they yelled. They danced about. They hugged each other. They laughed.

"Excuse me," came a voice. "Am I allowed to join in all this merriment?"

The Princess Bella peered down from the top of the mountain of treasure.

"Oh, Princess, dear Bella, forgive me," cried Ned. "Why, if it hadn't been for you and that wonderful ball throwing, we would never have defeated the dragon. You were brilliant!"

Ned started to climb up the pile. As he did so, the treasure gave a lurch and began to topple.

"Oh no, Ned," cried Bella. "Careful! I'll be left hanging by the cord!"

Ned scrambled up a little higher but the pile shifted and tipped, and a cascade of shiny things started to slip and tumble downwards. As he looked up, he saw Bella's chair plunge a little further. She clung there, a nervous look in her eyes, her hand raised towards the ceiling with the cord. But as he watched, he saw the cord loosen. It uncoiled itself like a small snake and fell from the ring in the ceiling. Simultaneously it unwound itself from Bella's wrist. Then it fell, shrivelled, to the floor.

But by now the impetus of the shifting objects was causing a little landslide, and the caskets, the jewels, the bright fabric, the gold and silver all started to topple downwards. Bella fell too, her dress flying out behind her. Ned was ahead of her, tumbling head-over-heels. He landed with a bump on the floor and, looking up, saw Bella hurtling down towards him.

Crash! She landed on him, and for a moment they lay sprawled together on the floor as a shower of jewels and treasure clattered about them. Ned jumped to his feet and helped up the princess. And there she was, looking at his embarrassed face, a smile on hers. She rubbed her wrist where the green cord had been tied, and they stood for a moment staring at each other.

Then she spoke. "You did it, Ned. You killed

the dragon and saved me. Thank you."

Their hands came together, and they stood gazing at each other in wonder and delight. Then Tuff gave an impatient grunt.

"Blow me, Ned, boy!" he said. "Don't you think it's time to get out of here? We've done more than our dooty, if you asks me! Time to go home."

"Oh yes," said Dilly. "Let's go home, dear boy." And Ned put his arms around her neck and hugged her. There was nothing he would've liked better.

"I suppose we go down the tunnel," he said. "Lead on, Rabbit."

Rabbit and his family ran ahead and disappeared. The mice scampered after and all the others started to follow. Bella bent down and picked up her golden ball, but as she did so, a huge rumbling noise like cracking thunder echoed through the mountain. The whole craggy rock was crumbling about them!

HOMEWARD

WITH THE DRAGON'S DEATH, THE MAGIC OF THE DARK MOUNTAIN WAS BROKEN. Fearfully they watched as the floor of the cave cracked open. Suddenly it gave way and they moved with it. They were part of the rock, part of the very mountain, and they slid downwards with the landslide around them. The dragon's lair was destroyed before their very eyes, and all its treasure was buried in the dust and rubble.

Ned, Bella and the animals found themselves lying at the foot of the crag, dazed but miraculously unharmed.

As they looked about them, they saw that the sky was bathed in a pale light. And then it was

as if the skies had opened: a downpour of rain
soaked into the parched landscape, finding its
way into cracks and dry, rocky seams and filling
them all with fresh water. Ned and Bella raised
their faces to the rain. As they watched, the
heavy fog that had lain for so long over the land
disappeared, and they could see blue sky.

Then, through all the rain, the sun started to
shine. As they looked up, they saw five magpies
fly towards them over the rubble. In their beaks
some had bits of treasure they had pilfered from
the treasure chamber as it crumbled down. They
flew ahead, cackling.

"We always knew you
could do it!" called
the biggest bird.

"Mind you, you
took your time
about it!" called
another. They
cackled with laughter.

"Those dreadful birds," said Tuff in fury. "Always on the lookout for what they can get."

"Where were you when we needed some help?" called Ned, but the magpies were too busy with their glittering objects to reply, and off they flew.

Tuff leaped up at them, yapping.

"Let them go, Tuff," said Bella. "Some creatures are always trouble."

Tired but full of relief, the friends gazed at the landscape ahead of them.

"Walk on, Dilly," said Ned. "Ready, Tuff?"

"Ready as I'll ever be, Ned, lad." The little dog trotted up beside Dilly. "Ta-ta, Rabbit. I'm very sorry about our little mix-up earlier. Thanks for all your help."

The rabbit stood on his hind legs, his whiskers twitching. "Never thought I'd be saying a fond farewell to a dog and a fox, but farewell. Farewell to all of you." He hopped off and nibbled at the grass. "Perhaps we'll get a bit of peace now," his relatives muttered as they hopped after him.

So off they went – a boy, a princess, a pony, a little dog, a pig, an otter, a lark, a mouse and all the brave animals who had come to help Ned. It was a joyous journey this time, full of triumph instead of dread.

"Did you see how I tackled that old dragon!" Tuff was saying to any listening animal. "I . . . er . . . I mean, we showed it what's what and no mistake!" His tail wagged and wagged.

All along their route, the friends were greeted by animals lining the wayside and cheering. One by one, the animals who had come to their help in the cave left the procession to join those at the wayside, and Bella earnestly thanked them all. Now only the original members of the "princess's army" remained, but still, with every step they took, creatures came to cheer, calling out, "Hooray for the Princess Bella! Hooray for Butterfingers!"

Gradually they saw the bleached land on either side start to change. It was as if the earth breathed once more. Around them green grass rose up; flowers sprang forth under Dilly's hooves; birds filled the new blue of the sky, swallows flashing across their gaze. The air was fresh once more, sweetened by the smell of blossom. New leaves opened up on the trees, green and lush. The animals who lined the way threw flowers at them. Ned put them in his hat and on Dilly's bridle, and Bella stuck them in her hair. They looked around joyfully at the brightening land.

As they descended the foothills, they heard the trill of birds, and Lark swooped down to Ned.

"It's my family greeting me! Oh, it's good to be back. Farewell, you brave and foolish . . . er . . . you brave boy," she said. "And if you're ever this way again, listen out for me."

At the dark wood, Foxy grinned and saluted them. "An interesting excursion, dear boy," he said. "One so likes a change now and again. A delightfully unexpected little adventure."

"It's you who were unexpected, Foxy," said Ned.

"I'd never have guessed you'd be such a help in my time of need. I thank you with all my heart."

"Wouldn't have missed it, dear boy. Wouldn't have missed it for anything. Not only was it entertaining, it was the first time that I've had so much co-operation from a dog." He tilted his head musingly and grinned. "It will no doubt be my last. I wish you and the lady all the best, Ned. A fond farewell to you all."

"Never thought I'd trust a fox, but it just shows – you never can tell," said Tuff.

They came to the cornfield and Mouse jumped off Ned's shoulder and down onto a corn stalk.

"Home," she squeaked. "Not that I didn't enjoy my temporary stay in your jerkin, Ned. You never know, I might move a little closer to the palace and come and visit."

"Please do, Mouse."

How strange it was, that trip homewards. As if by magic, the long, long journey back seemed to take no time at all. What had taken days and nights, with heavy hearts, on the way to the dragon's lair, now seemed to pass by quickly and easily. Before they knew it, they were near the otter's home.

"You helped us find the way, and you gave me courage," said Ned, standing on the bridge and looking down at the river. "I'll never forget you, Otter."

"None of us will," said the princess.

So they went onwards on the final part of their journey.

SAFE

WHEN THEY NEARED THE RUN-DOWN FARM WHERE PIGGY LIVED, HE TROTTED TO THE GATE, LOOKING THROUGH AT HIS OLD STY. He gave a wistful grunt.

"Funny, isn't it?" he said. "At one time all I wanted was to eat and roll in my mud, but I don't know – it's lost some of its charm."

"Piggy," said Ned, "you're coming back with us. You were the first one to come on the journey with us, the first one to help us. You'll stay with us – is that all right, my lady?"

"You are definitely coming back to the palace with us, Piggy dear," said Bella.

Tuff grinned widely. "It'll be good to have you nearby, old mate," he said. "And the first thing we'll do is get you a big meal."

"Now you're talking," said Piggy. "I've been more than a little peckish for far too long." He quickened his pace at the thought of food.

"And we'll give you a nice sty near the stables," said Ned. "One with plenty of mud."

So the friends set off on the last lap of their journey. Finally they saw before them the king's palace. As they neared it, the gates opened, and to Ned's surprise a crowd of people ran out to greet them, cheering wildly. He felt quite overwhelmed and wondered if he should slip off. The crowd parted to allow the king to come forward, tears in his eyes, to meet his beloved daughter.

Bella ran up to her father. They embraced each other as if they would never let go and

then made their way through the crowds
across the old familiar ground.

Ned took Dilly's bridle and led her off towards
her stall.

"Don't go, Ned," called Bella. "Wait, I'll come
with you."

Together they went into the stables – the place
where Ned and Dilly and Tuff had spent so many
years. But it was also the place where Ned worked.
He looked around, suddenly a little nervous.

There was Squelch, standing in his large leather
apron, his dirty wide-brimmed hat in his hand,
familiar grumpy expression on his face. Ned
felt slightly uneasy, but it was Squelch who bent
his head this time. His eyes flickered up to look
uncertainly at his old stable lad. He was unsure
whether to order him to "get in here quick, boy"
or to bow.

Although some had perished, many of the old
horses had returned to the stables, carrying their
knights away from the terrible mountain crag

and the dragon's fire. They raised their heads and neighed in welcome. Ned led Dilly to her old stall in the corner, followed by Bella.

"Master Squelch," she called out in her clear voice, "this pony, Dilly, is to be given the very best stall, worthy of a champion charger. She is to be given your finest oats. And Ned's heroic pet dog, Tuff, is to be given a hearty meal and warm bedding. These two are valiant members of the king's court and must be treated as such."

Tuff stared at her open-mouthed. Then his tail started to wag violently but he sat down quickly to hide it. "Oh, yeah? Member of the court – well, it's only to be expected. Knew it would happen sooner or later." And in a show of nonchalance he started to scratch.

Bella and Ned laughed.

Squelch rushed off to prepare the stall; Ned made as if to help, but Bella stopped him.

"As for Ned," she announced to the crowd, "he is a knight worthy of any princess, for he has saved me. He has saved us all."

"Ned will no longer be a stableboy," said the king, joining his daughter, "but a knight. He'll be given a suit of armour and a sword of his own. And he will be called Sir Ned."

What? Sir Ned? It seemed far too grand. Ned opened his mouth to say so, but the king went on:

"Ned, and his dog, Tuff, and his pony, Dilly, have saved our kingdom."

The crowd cheered. Ned looked around at them, shy and embarrassed. He saw Squelch frowning and made out the fat shape of the cook, who was saying to her neighbour: "I always liked that boy. I was always very fond of that one, you know." Ned smiled to himself, remembering how very fond she was of clouting him.

Then, among the crowd, Ned saw the knights who had returned from the mountain – the pompous Sir Fayn, the fat Sir Belwyn, who had been so keen to shout orders; and some younger knights, who looked at Ned and smiled. Would he really be one of them?

Bella suddenly left her father's side and made her way over to Ned, who was standing back, holding Dilly's bridle. Tuff ran forward, his tail wagging. The princess bent down and patted his head and stroked Dilly's nose. Then she went up to Ned, leaned forward and kissed him on the cheek. Ned forgot his worries. He looked at her and smiled. Then she took both his hands in hers and leaned forward once more. And this time, with her eyes shining brightly, she tipped her head and quickly kissed his mouth.

"That's my Ned!" yapped Tuff, leaping in the air with his little legs. "Ain't he a wonder? That's my boy!"

"He's always been a good boy, my Ned,"

murmured Dilly quietly. "And good boys get their rewards – haven't I always said so?"

"Far too often, you silly mare, but it seems you was right for once!"

Bella laughed, and ran off. Then she stopped and turned round to look at Ned.

"Come on," she said. From the pocket of her dress she took her golden ball and tossed it to him. Up went Ned's hands to catch it, but it slipped from his grasp and rolled onto the ground. He blushed, as usual, and ran to pick it up as it rolled away.

"Butterfingers," the princess said with a grin.

Then she gave a loud, delighted laugh.
"Sir Butterfingers!"
Ned stood tall. He felt full of joy. How could he ever have minded such a name?
All around him the crowd cheered delightedly.

"Sir Butterfingers!"
they cried.